What this shit is a

Semi-naked women

Armor-plated muscle cars

Funky attitudes

Shotguns

Pimp slapping

Backstabbing

Bloodthirsty housewives

Greed

Sex

Sharp teeth

The players...

Marley
The expediter. The thinking man's
roughneck in a Hugo Boss suit

Lina Guzmán
The fine-ass drug cartel queen
who doesn't take shit from anyone

Samson Twelvetrees
The duplicitous lieutenant out to kill Lina
no matter what it takes

Dakin Saunders
The ambitious California Attorney General

The Furys
Bad babes with big guns

The Goth Hit Team
Murderous dime store bloodsuckers

Coleridge
The lascivious defrocked doc

Plus an assortment of thugs and shooters
looking to get paid by making sure Marley and
Ms. Guzmán never reach their goal alive

The Perpetrators

Gary Phillips

UglyTown
Los Angeles

First Edition

Text copyright © 2002 by Gary Phillips. All Rights Reserved.
Art copyright © 2002 by Paul Pope. All Rights Reserved.

UGLYTOWN AND THE UGLYTOWN COIN LOGO SERVICEMARK REG. U.S. PAT. OFF.

Library of Congress Card Catalog Number: 2001096415

ISBN: 0-9663473-7-4

Find out more of the mystery: UglyTown.com/Perps

Printed in the United States of America

10 9 8 7 6 5 4 3 2 1

To the storytellers:
Big John Buscema, Gil Kane,
and Budd Boetticher

The
Perpetrators

"The only conception I can have is that of the prisoner or the individual in the midst of the State. The only one I know is freedom of thought and action."

—Albert Camus

7:48am
Tijuana, Mexico

The hunting knife swept down toward the skull of the fly black man in the di Marco suit. His game face on, Marley blocked the overhand thrust with his forearm.

"*Pinche cabrón,*" the knife man groaned, then made a vicious jab at brother man's gut.

Marley threw his body out of the doorway and into the room, narrowly avoiding the blade. Behind him and the bed, Lina Guzmán leveled her Beretta at the assassin.

"No," Marley hissed, his back against the funky wallpaper. "No shots, or we got 5-o."

The hombre with the knife stepped in close, waving his pig sticker back and forth. The steely tip whisked past Marley's Armani shirt, slicing a button off as he twisted aside. A tight smile creased his rugged face. "That's your ass, *amigo,* you don't fuck with my gear."

The knife man frowned, "*No habla Inglés.*"

"*Habla* this, motherfuckah."

Marley popped off a kick, the man's mouth spouting crimson. The knife man buckled. Marley followed up with the style he employed best, street fighting. He set up the chump with two rapid lefts and dropped him with a straight right.

Woozy, the knife handler's agape mouth revealed two gold front teeth as he struggled to his knees. His eyes focused as he peeped Lina Guzmán securing a suppressor to her Beretta. In a fluid motion she let off two hot ones, wetting the knife man's chest. He keeled over.

He wouldn't be getting up anymore.

"No noise, no cops, no problems," Guzmán said.

She was up against it, but would be damned if she'd have anybody tag her as helpless.

Marley allowed a nod. *Welcome to Tijuana, now get the fuck out.* He eyeballed the raggedy hotel room with its rabbit-eared television playing a soap opera silently, faded paisley wallpaper, nasty-ass shag carpeting, and the smell of lost hope. It was only eight in the morning, but the heat outside already made the room oppressive.

Marley had been in worse, a hell of a lot worse. But this was no time to reminisce about parachuting in from 25,000 feet, part of a 12-man detachment, and all the crazy shit he'd been through back in his Special Ops days.

Taking a moment to clean blood from the tip of his Mezlan shoe, Marley gave his full attention to his latest client. She coldly replaced her gun in the conceal-and-carry in the waistband of her Versace capri pants. She was long and tall and slim-waisted with enough upstairs and down to keep things interesting. If not for her attitude—which had been evident in their phone conversation—she might have been all that. As it was, he was sure she'd prove to be a pain in the ass. But so what? Those ducats she was lacing him down with were worth the stress. Hopefully.

"You fucked up," Marley snapped as he strode to the open door and glanced in both directions along the hallway. Only the muffled sounds of a couple slappin' skin could be heard a few doors down in room 14.

"I fucked up?" Guzmán rasped. "I told you I was in danger."

7:50am

"You're going to be in a lot more danger if you don't do as I say," he said. "Your boy Samson Twelvetrees is gonna have shooters coming at us like flies on stink from here 'til we light up north. That's 600 miles of potential death unless you get on the good foot."

Marley eased the door shut and crouched next to the dead man. He began rifling through his pockets.

"You can't talk to me like that." She put her hands on rounded hips, her eyes dark and hard. "Not with what I'm paying you."

"How should I talk to you, Ms. Guzmán? You called me, I didn't call you. You need me, I don't need you." He kept searching.

She folded her arms and tapped a foot. "Whatevah ..."

Marley grunted. His research on Lina Guzmán had informed him she was the only heir to one of the biggest drug operations Columbia had ever produced. She'd inherited Arturo Rosalva Guzmán's business and ran it like a machine. Twenty years ago her pops had been a chemist at a soap company. When he got tired of chump change, he applied his knowledge of formulas to get his cut of that South American country's number one export: cocaine. He worked smart and, by many accounts, ruthlessly. Rewarded for his efforts, he built an empire on snow.

Two years ago, after his violent departure from this world, his daughter transformed an already substantial empire into the Microsoft of the dope trade.

Marley shifted his orderly mind back to the task at hand while he stood and examined what he found. There were a set of keys, a pair of gaffs—hooks used on fighting cocks—a Los Tigres Del Norte cassette, and a ballpoint pen.

"You sure you can get me there alive?" Guzmán paced back and forth, stopping only to peer out the window at the bus station across the Rio Zonal thoroughfare. "I am

paying you $350,000 down against a sweet two million to get—"

"Your tight ass to Sacramento by four tomorrow," he finished for her. "I don't need reminding." The icy-demeanored black man smoothed out his Steven Land tie.

"You're a prick."

"Save your jaw-jacking in case we get jammed by the Border Patrol. Things are a lot tighter these days, you know." He saw that the pen was from Le Colonial, a touristy hotel in Tijuana. He put that and the gaffs into his inner suit pocket.

"Let's bounce. And you can leave the Louis V. behind." Marley pointed to the two suitcases. Her mouth was working, and he held up a hand to cut the static. "There could be tracking devices sewn into their linings. Twelvetrees has got a real hard-on to take over your shit and take you out. And he won't stop."

"What do I do for clothes? I like to look good—I am *La Reina* after all." She'd put the girly-girl in her voice to get him sprung.

There was no doubt she was fine, but his mind and body were in offensive mode.

"You'll get by."

7:55am

He opened the door and scoped the empty hallway again. The couple in room 14 were going at it like they'd invented fuckin', then abruptly halted—a little too quick. His radar kicked into high.

Motioning Guzmán back into the room, he walked down the hallway's dingy carpet toward the room. "Yeah, we'll take the train to La Jolla and switch there," he said loud enough for anyone in 14 to hear.

The door to the room banged open, and a red-haired Latina burst into the hall. Under other circumstances Marley would be vibin' on her painted lips, big titties, and black sheer panties covering a jigglin' ass. But dual machetes had a peculiar way of narrowing his attention. Big Red also had on an Aztec headdress and twirled those bad boys like a pro.

A whirlwind of steel, she advanced on Marley. He rarely broke an emotion, but even he had to show this honey some respect. He set himself, focusing on what he had to do or get sliced and diced.

Naturally Guzmán had disobeyed him and was now in the hallway. She didn't have her gun out, and if she reached for it now, Big Red would lop her head off. The woman in the headdress grinned, showing bad teeth. He inserted himself between her and his client.

Marley feinted left at the precise millisecond that Big Red took a swipe, one of the deadly instruments whispering past his face. She chopped with the other one, but he spun, his reverse kick catching the redhead in her face. She reeled back and swung again, both machetes whisking past the top of his head as he ducked. Marley planted a hard blow in her stomach that caused her to drop one of the machetes. She tried to nut him with the other one, but he grabbed her wrist and broke it effortlessly.

Big Red yelped, "Sonofbit—" He finished her with a modified backhand strike that knocked the *loca mujer* out.

Guzmán said to him, "Not bad. Maybe I should have

listened to you, and met you at the safe house in Baja like you'd suggested."

Yeah, she was going to be a treasure. Through the open door to 14 Marley spotted Big Red's former love interest, a naked fat fool, a bowler atop his curly locks. The mark was beached on his back atop a grubby comforter, his Columbian necktie sprouting fresh blood from ear-to-ear.

Marley dragged Big Red into the room. Using an electrical cord from a lamp, he hogtied the woman. He tossed her in bed with the dead man and closed the door.

Marley and Guzmán turned to leave. They had transportation to catch at the TJ bus station.

Guzmán said, "I think I've seen enough of Tijuana for one day."

*   *   *

Samson Twelvetrees enjoyed having his dick sucked on the regular, morning, noon, and night. He particularly liked having a kneeling ash blonde amazon in five-inch fuck-me shoes and a thong do it just like Stella, or whatever the hell was her name, was doing now. Like ex-president Clinton, he liked getting head while he took care of business. Sitting sideways at his chrome office desk in his Armani silk robe, he leaned back in his padded swivel as the blonde worked his rod.

His angular bronze face, a mix of Slavic and Asiatic Indian features, was enigmatically composed. He was a Charles Bronson for the new millennium.

"Is that right?" he said into the handset. "I am disappointed to hear they got away."

8:23am

Impassively he listened to the caller from Tijuana. "I see," Twelvetrees eventually remarked. "You have them tailed on the bus, that's good. Get our next team ready in

San Diego. I'm sure this Marley, this *caballero* who calls himself an expediter, will get them off the bus there and switch to a car or truck."

He was about to hang up but then added, "And let's do it right this time, understand? That frosty ho is not to get to Sacramento and meet with Saunders." He laughed. "I want her guts in a sack so I can feed them to my Rottweilers."

He hung up, and his eyes fluttered with pleasure as he let loose in whatshername's mouth.

8:31am

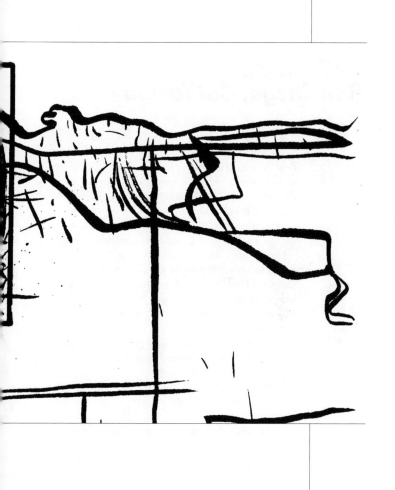

10:42am
San Diego, California

Marley and his charge crossed the expanse of El Cajon Boulevard as all manner of vehicles drove by. He'd gotten them off the bus in downtown San Diego. He'd suspected the kid with the boombox sitting two rows behind them was a tail, but the non-stop trip hadn't afforded him an opportunity to sweat the little shit. The kid had stayed on the bus, but Marley was sure he'd called in their position.

They got to a side street which contained industrial-style structures. He pointed at their destination, a low-slung, red brick building down the block. Cut-out metal letters, 12-feet high, proclaiming the establishment as MILLAR PERFUME DISTRIBUTORS stood upright like sentinels on the roof.

"You sure know how to show a girl the town, player."

He ignored her sarcasm and continued walking, nearing a wooden fence.

Plastered in a row along the fence were campaign posters picturing California Attorney General Dakin Saunders.

"Your savior," he remarked caustically, indicating the broadsides.

"Fuck that. You never had to make a choice you couldn't live with, Marley?"

"Once or twice."

Saunders was an arch-conservative family values cheer-leader. When the horrible events of the WTC and the Pentagon happened, he'd intimated on a radio call-in show that America, home to lip-pierced lesbians and the ACLU, got what it deserved. Later, under intense pressure from the state Legislature, he "modified" his remarks. In his campaign posters, the asshole wore the same expression he always did—like he had a plunger handle up his ass. By making a deal with Guzmán, he would build up his standing in the polls in his bid for governor. And she got immunity.

"Come on," Marley said, pushing open the glass door.

"Hi," the beach bunny hottie in the slit mini at the reception desk greeted him. "Trap has it ready."

"Thanks, Dora." Marley walked up to a locked door at the rear of the room. As Guzmán followed, she noticed the bulky Desert Eagle Dora tucked away under her desk as she reached into a drawer.

"Here, let's get you into a fresh one." She extracted a folded and pressed Hugo Boss slate blue Oxford shirt. Dora stood and touched the area on Marley's shirt where the button was missing.

"Why not?"

Dora helped him out of his jacket and loosened his tie. She also slipped him out of his shoulder holster with the S&W 945 combat model automatic in the rig. Then she began to unbutton his shirt, pulling it loose from around his taut waist.

"Oh, please," Guzmán said.

"He's got to represent, Ms. Guzmán." Dora winked at her.

10:59am

Guzmán looked annoyed but checked out Marley's V'd upper body and his rigid six pack. He wasn't short, nor was he that tall. He couldn't have been more than a year or two older than her twenty-seven, but there was a thin zigzag of white shot through the top part of his close-cropped hair. And she'd seen enough bullet holes to recognize a couple of healed wounds on his torso, along with numerous scars. He'd been through a lot. But then, so had she.

"Much better," Dora murmured, after getting the new shirt on him and knotting his tie. One of her hands rested on his pecs.

"Full of surprises, aren't you?" Guzmán chided.

"Ain't I," he answered. He rolled up the cuffs, putting his silver Cartier cuff links in his pocket.

Guzmán was surprised he didn't have a Baume & Mercier or similar expensive timepiece on his wrist. Rather, it was a beat Elgin with a cracked leather band. Some kind of family keepsake, she surmised.

Marley punched in a combination on an electronic key pad. The rear door swung outward, and the duo entered the main area of the building. Inside, several men and women went about the routine of boxing and shipping fancy bottles and jars of scented water. A tall, stocky

black man with a twenty-two-inch neck and arms the size of a bull's leg hanging out of a grease-stained tank top appeared before them.

"Stone Cold Marley," the man said.

"Trap." Marley shook his hand, his coat draped over an arm. "What do you have for me, brah?"

"Self-sealing tires, LTA glass, Armormax undercarriage, night vision navigator, and some goodies in the hide-away." He tossed Marley the keys.

"Lead on."

The three walked into another space in the rear. Profiled in subdued lighting was a '73 black Dodge Charger with gleaming Dayton rims.

"Well?" Trap jabbed a thumb in the direction of the ride.

"It'll do." Marley opened the door and put his coat on the back seat.

Trap addressed Guzmán. "That's as close to a compliment I've ever gotten out of this cat."

"He must really like you."

Marley opened the trunk and took inventory. In short order, he closed the lid. "If anybody comes around—"

"They're already dealt with," Trap finished.

Marley unlatched the passenger door. "If you please, Ms. Guzmán."

The big man undid a padlock on a corrugated metal garage door and worked the chain to raise it.

Marley eased the finely-tuned hemi monster onto the street, looking everywhere as he slipped the Hurst shifter

into first. Soon he had the car into higher gear, heading north along the 5 Freeway. Methodically, he checked the rearview and side mirrors.

11:37am

"Relax, who's going to find us now?" Guzmán reached for the radio.

Marley blared, "Don't play that."

Defiantly, she turned the Blaupunkt up as a rap song blazed. "What's wrong, Marley, afraid you might slip and let a twitch show?" She bopped her head to the sounds.

"If a vehicle is moving up on us, I want to hear it. Stop acting like a brat." He turned the knob and the decibels dropped.

She flashed him the finger. "Fuck you. You're getting plenty of *feria* and I have to put up with your bullshit rules? What I say," she poked him in the chest, "goes. *Entiéndase?*"

Okay, she was used to running a multi-million-dollar empire, used to fools cracking the ceiling when she said jump. But that didn't mean shit to him. Marley didn't like to repeat himself, so he didn't. Sooner than later, though, he was gonna have to put this chick who blew hot and cold in check.

The car picked up speed and Marley zoomed around a pick-up with a surfboard hanging out its bed. What the hell, now was a good time to press his point. He drove off the side of the road into weeds. "Go on, get to steppin'."

Guzmán aimed the Beretta at his eye. "Drive, mother-fuckah."

11:39am

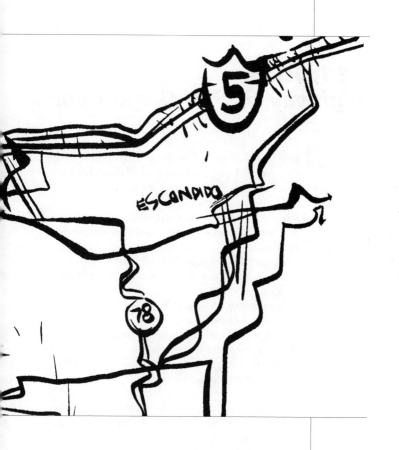

Lina Guzmán had to show she couldn't be bossed. Sure, she needed Marley, but her father had taught her you had to be ruthless—you had to set the limits.

"If you bad, pull the trigger." Marley's face remained impassive, his voice a rusty scalpel scraped across stone. The barrel of the Beretta was less than an inch from his right eye.

She smiled. "You don't think I'll peel your cap?"

An urgent look now lit his features. "That pick-up," he said in a quiet voice.

Guzmán wasn't buying. "Come off it, Marley. You have to kiss my ass now."

His hand became a blur as he snatched the gun away from her. She stared at him, stunned. Marley was already guiding the Charger back into the flow of traffic. Then he got that familiar tickle in his brain.

"That pick-up with the surfboard we just went by on the freeway is the same one that passed us on El Cajon less than an hour ago. Then it had tools in the bed. But I remember the dented rear bumper."

She sneered. "Your security mania has become paranoia, Marley."

"We'll see." Contemptuously, he tossed the gun back to her.

She looked at the gat as if it were a giant bug. "You're one crazy *bendejo*."

Marley drove faster, taking the middle lane, watching and waiting. Ahead was a semi. And in front of that was the pick-up. He slowed down, hoping to keep pace with the smaller truck. But he also figured the pick-up was the lookout vehicle. And that whoever was driving it had to be talking to the attack car.

"You might just get a chance to use that heater again, Lil' Kim." He adjusted the rearview mirror.

"Fuck you and your mama." Despite her words, she tried to suppress the arousing nervousness overtaking her. She studied Marley, his taut frame, aware that her eyes were on him too long. Guzmán shifted in the seat, making an effort to glare out the windshield.

"Here they come," Marley warned, glancing back over his shoulder.

A Mazda MPV family van suddenly detached itself from the rest of the cars behind them and came up steadily from the left lane.

"This might be the decoy, but roll up your window anyway."

She did. Marley held his speed steady. The van was a car length back, and they both studied the driver. The woman piloting the vehicle was middle-aged and heavy-set, with her hair in curlers. The van leaped forward, keeping pace with the Charger. Marley hit a switch and the back seat dropped down as he guided the car into the fast lane.

11:46am

"About time," Guzmán said, eyeing the array of firepower he'd revealed.

The pick-up was still ahead of them. Now the van, too, moved slightly ahead. The woman brought her passenger window down and leveled a Tec-9 on Marley. He didn't flinch as she dashed off rounds from the pistol. The hollow points caused small spider webs in the bullet-proof glass.

Marley dropped his foot on the accelerator, and the three-and-half-ton-plus car with its big block 492 tore past the van with ease. Deftly, he moved in and out of traffic, easily avoiding a bus load of children.

"Careful," Guzmán clipped, watching them leave the kids behind.

So she did think about more than just herself, Marley noted. The van and pick-up truck were now one behind the other on the inside lane. Marley slowed down, letting a station wagon go by. He jerked the steering wheel and cut across to the middle lane again as the eighteen wheeler barreled up. The Charger was mere inches from being creamed.

"Shit!" Guzmán shouted, digging her purple-nailed hand into Marley's arm.

The truck's air horn bellowed as the driver rode the brakes, his tires smoking. Guzmán swore again, and Marley gritted his teeth, the semi's bumper thudding against theirs. He gunned the engine and twisted the wheel. The truck clipped the car's rear panel.

"Oh shit, oh shit!" Guzmán yelled.

The Charger went up a hillock of sage and fishtailed onto a dirt roadway, but Marley righted it, shooting plumes of dust. The truck kept going, but several cars had slammed into each other trying to avoid an accident.

Guzmán was turned around in her seat, taking in the scene. "We still have company."

"Get that Browning auto loose."

Guzmán pulled the shotgun and shells from the rack of weapons. She sat down and checked the gun to make sure it was primed.

Out of the corner of his eye, Marley caught her expert handling of the piece. "So, you are good for something."

Guzmán gave him a look and rolled her window down.

She got in position on her knees, leaning out the window to be able to point and shoot. "Come on, player, don't just drool over my butt." She looked over her shoulder at Marley.

"I'm all business."

"Right."

The pick-up had juice under the hood. It shot forward, two men in it, the passenger firing an AK-47. Guzmán ducked back inside the armor-protected car. Marley hooked a vicious right just as the truck pulled close.

"Now."

Guzmán poked her body out again and cranked off blasts at the pick-up's windshield. The glass burst and the passenger grabbed at his face, screaming. The driver was also cut, but he kept the vehicle on course.

Marley whipped the steering wheel around in a tire-screeching donut. The pick-up was now in front and the Charger behind.

"Your girlfriend's joining the party," Guzmán said.

The MPV van was bouncing over the terrain, kicking up clouds.

"Concentrate on these two first." Marley was chasing the pick-up. The road forked, and the two vehicles went right, parallel to a field of tomatoes. The pick-up took a sharp turn and cut through part of the vegetable patch. Marley closed in.

The passenger popped up, his face a mess of red trailings. He fired his assault weapon through the truck's back window, decimating it. The rounds blistered against the Charger's windshield. Marley breathed in and poured it on. The van pulled closer still.

11:49am

The pick-up tried to veer off, but the Charger was too fast. Marley rammed the rear quarter panel of the truck, sending it skidding. An explosion went off behind the Charger.

"Fuck!" Guzmán turned around. "Look what she's

using now. I've seen the FARC guerillas back home with those."

"An M-79 grenade launcher, or a variation of one." Marley gave the car more pedal. He maneuvered the Charger out of the way just as the woman let loose with another grenade. The projectile didn't make a direct hit, but the concussion knocked out the glass on the Charger's passenger side.

"Come on, Marley," Guzmán said, hitting his arm. "You supposed to be all that."

"Yeah, yeah." His snarl blended with the sound of the winding torque on the clutch. "You have to take out the truck, *comprende?*"

"*Si se puede*, as they say on the picket line, homey."

The deadly soccer mom was taking aim again with her cannon. Marley put the hammer down, and the car leapt, slipping right behind the pick-up. All three vehicles veered around each other, over small hills and ruts bounded by swaths of farmland. The Charger rammed the rear end of the small truck.

"Watch out," Guzmán said.

The gunner in the pick-up was firing again, but Marley had counted on this. He downshifted and simultaneously cranked the steering wheel to the left, turning away. The car's front end shuddered violently.

The assault weapon raked the side of the Charger and clipped part of the van. The woman had also turned off to avoid being shot.

"Good, she isn't armored." To Guzmán he said, "Get set." He brought the Charger side-by-side with the pick-up as the truck shot through a row of strawberries. Workers in the field scattered as the speeding vehicles tore through. The shooter attempted to blaze on the two but couldn't get an accurate shot past the driver.

"Steady, steady." Guzmán sighted along the Browning's barrel and pumped off blasts. Her shots were true, and the other driver's side window disappeared into thousands of glass snowflakes.

The pick-up went careening through the strawberry fields, a corpse at the wheel. The shooter tried to control the vehicle but got tangled up attempting to push the driver out of the truck. The vehicle slammed into an irrigation tank.

Marley was already rocking the Charger out of the rows of fruit, and the van was burning hot on his tire treads—the woman in curlers was relentless. She shot off another grenade. This one scored and blew out a section of the Charger's trunk and rear bumper.

Panic contorted Guzmán's face. "Earn your pay, Marley."

11:58am

"What do you think I'm doing, Ms. Guzmán," he said in a tight voice.

"Nothing much if I wind up on a slab." Taking shells from her pocket, she reloaded the shotgun, nervously dropping a couple of them.

They were now on a paved road that ran at a diagonal

away from the freeway. Peeling off the 5 toward the racing cars were three California Highway Patrol cars.

"Can things get any better?" Guzmán threw up her hands.

Marley bounced the Charger over low stumps of color-ful plants. He got to a rise, then brought the car around full circle. The van was bearing down on them, and the Chips were coming up strong behind the Mazda.

"Seat belts, kids." He gunned the Dodge straight for the van.

"Marley?" Guzmán put the lethal end of the shotgun against his ribs. "You better be bluffing."

"And you better drop that habit of pointing guns at me."

The woman in the van held her grenade launcher out-side the driver's window. She let off a grenade, but Marley had anticipated that and swerved out of its path. He then came back at her. The vehicles were less than fifteen yards apart. Marley understood this play required both hands on the wheel. Curlers put her toy away and got busy on her steering.

Guzmán screamed, "Turn this fucking car, Marley!"

Four yards and nothing left but guts. A light burned behind his eyes.

Guzmán's body was petrified with fright. The Charger didn't let up.

"Marley," she said, her breath trapped in her body.

His heart was racing faster than a thoroughbred, but he wasn't going to blink. Marley's hands were molded to the steering wheel, and his foot had the accelerator pushed to the floor. "Come on, you old broad, let's see what ya got."

At the last possible second, the van turned and careened off the side of the Charger. Both cars went out of control.

The veins stood out like cables on the backs of Marley's hands as he tried to right his muscle car. He succeeded, and the Charger zoomed past a grove of trees. One of the Highway Patrol cars was zeroing in on them.

"Oh shit." Guzmán glared behind her.

"Box. Open it."

She looked back at the cache of armaments and spotted the container.

"Today, while I'm young and good looking."

She fumbled with the lid, her hands shaking from the recent close call. She got it together and flipped the lid to reveal two plastic oval balloons held in place by brackets.

"Throw one behind us," Marley said, giving the engine all the car had left. The speedometer's needle vibrated at 135.

She got a balloon loose, leaned out the window, and threw it. The soft bomb exploded in a paroxysm of fire and heat.

Guzmán was knocked back into the seat, a shocked look on her face.

"Napalm," Marley said.

The driver of the Highway Patrol car had locked up his brakes and swerved in an effort to avoid incineration. The car rolled, and the two cops inside cursed loud and long as they flipped upside down into a carrot patch.

Marley screeched to a halt among a stand of maple trees.

"Move," he told Guzmán. He reached for a leather Dunhill attaché case in the compartment, taking his coat and the other napalm grenade.

She got out of the car, still holding the shotgun.

"Leave that. It's too conspicuous."

12:04pm

"You working my last good nerve, you know that?" She threw the shotgun into the car.

They got several yards from the Charger, and he pitched the balloon while they hit the dirt. The car went up. Even as embers billowed all about them, Marley was getting Guzmán to her feet and moving off.

"Let me guess, leave no fingerprints."

"No doubt."

The two disappeared into the wooded area. "We're not far from the private airport where I chartered a plane. We head over the mountains this way," Marley pointed, "and we're good to go. The *joota* will be too busy looking for us on the highway."

He started to head off, but Guzmán wasn't moving. He stopped, looking back at her.

"Hey!"

"I can't." She shook her head.

"Are you buggin'? We have to get movin', Ms. Guzmán."

"No planes, helicopters, gliders, anything that flies."

"What?" He was in her face.

"No," she repeated, stamping the ground like a 12-year-old who refused to eat spinach. "I won't fly."

Marley held out his arms, gesturing. "We can be in Sacramento in less than an hour and be done with this bullshit. I got mad safe places around there, and I get you to your appointment tomorrow when Saunders is back in town. Nobody will spot us, Lina. We won't get shot down."

"Forget it. You have to get me there on the ground." Defiantly, she glared up at him.

Marley tamped down his rising anger. He could put his barker on her, force her. But that seemed like an idea fraught with problems. He couldn't keep an eye on her like she was the enemy while he had beaucoup killers to deal with. She could handle a piece, and he was gonna need her skills if shit jumped off. *Analyze, man, analyze.*

"This has to do with how your father died, right?" he finally said.

Two years ago, *Señor* Guzmán's private Gulfstream had exploded in mid-air on its way to Miami. And that's when his daughter, who had been educated in Ivy League schools in the U.S. and had an MBA from Harvard, took over.

She nodded, holding herself.

Do like you been taught, Marley, improvise.

"Then we gotta hitchhike. But first we still have to go over these mountains to get away from the cops."

She jabbed a finger at him. "Just don't try anything funny."

He was going to be far too busy worrying about how vulnerable they would be on foot for anything else.

"Let's just book, aw'rite?"

The heat bore down on them as they made their way. Marley had Guzmán use his jacket to shield her head from the sun. Every now and then he'd put the attaché case on his head to block the harsh rays. They went on, thirsty and uncomfortable, their clothes sticking to them like grimy second skin.

12:49pm

"Can't we rest again?" she asked as they trudged down the other side of the mountains.

"No. We keep moving, and we're less likely to get tagged."

She grumbled, "I know you're just doing this to punish me."

"You act like I think this is a good time," he managed

between parched lips. "Because of you, I've got to redo my plans. I'll take us to the coast, then back inland, all the time getting us further north."

"I'm sorry, I just—"

"Save it."

Marley and Guzmán finally arrived in the scenic town of Carlsbad just past two in the afternoon, their bodies thick with dried, greasy sweat. They'd had to walk through the heat until getting back to the highway and lucked into catching a ride. She blew kisses at the Marines who'd given them a lift. They whooped and drove off in their bucket of a '72 Thunderbird.

"I've got to get some clothes. These rags are baked on me." Guzmán glared at him, expecting opposition.

"Fine," Marley said, sounding tired himself. Maybe he should never have taken this job with this whack chick. But he was in it and wasn't about to let go now. His work was him, and that meant it wasn't done on the half-step. Obstacles were only things to be overcome.

They got clothes from a secondhand store and put their dirty ones in a shopping bag. Then the pair got food and lodging at a rundown two-story joint called the Poseidon Motel not far from the ocean. It had rooms off an open courtyard. He paid and got the key.

"One room only, Mr. Marley?" Lina Guzmán wondered aloud.

"All the better to watch you, Ms. Guzmán," he replied in a monotone. "I can assure you, I won't be up to anything."

"Should I be insulted?"

He betrayed nothing. They went inside.

She stretched out on the bed. Sitting cross-legged with his back to the door, Marley opened the attaché case he'd brought with him. He checked his S&W, a cell phone, a pair of Dipol D2V night vision goggles, a wallet with cash, credit cards in someone else's name, and several fake driver's licenses. There was also a lock picking kit and several metallic disks the size of silver dollars, only thicker.

She watched with interest. "Don't you ever relax, Marley?"

He closed the case. "When I'm not clockin'." He rested the back of his head against the door.

"I see." She got off the bed, unbuttoning her blouse. "I'm going to take a shower." She took off her shirt slowly, revealing her black lace butterfly bra.

Marley betrayed little on his face, but his eyes glittered. She stepped closer to him, letting the garment fall to the floor.

"A lot of men would slap their mama upside the head to be in a motel room with me, Marley."

"I'm not a lot of men, Ms. Guzmán." He stood, their breaths intermingling. "And you can't buy my loyalty with pussy." A beat, then, "I'll get the job done, *chica*."

"Bastard."

"That's how you like 'em."

Before she could respond, the room's window disintegrated into a sparkling array of glass particles.

4:21pm

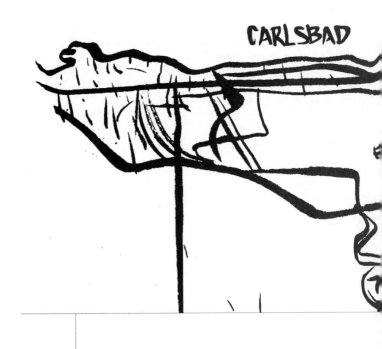

CARLSBAD

4:22pm
Carlsbad

A metal canister tumbled through the hole in the busted window. The thing rolled and emitted a purplish gas that sucked the air from the room.

Marley was already moving, handing Guzmán her blouse. "Put this over your nose."

"What good is that going to do with poison gas?"

"It's not meant to kill us, only drive us into the open like sheep." He knew the casing of the smoke device was designed to get hot, so he didn't waste time trying to pick it up or kick it.

She put the shirt to her face. "What do we do?" Her Beretta was in her hand.

Marley was in combat mode. He used his jacket to flap at the fumes. As he did this, he sensed more than saw an indistinct form moving at them through the smoke. He let off three rounds to back the intruder the fuck up, then tackled Guzmán. Return bursts of silenced bullets ripped into the bed and walls.

Pressed down on the floor behind the bed, Marley slipped on the night vision goggles. The specially coated luminescent lenses gave him greater clarity in the manufactured fog. He cranked off two more shots at the shape, now near the bathroom. The figure retreated.

"Come on." He got up, tugging on Guzmán's elbow.

Outside, two women in retro pop-glam attire surveyed the results of their handiwork.

One of the brickhouses was black, in butt-hugging hot pants with a large bubble afro. She wore an eyepatch on the left side of her face and hefted an HK SL8-1 assault rifle.

The second hammer was white, blonde, hair in little girl ponytails, wearing a clinging leather mid-thigh skirt with a slit up the side. She displayed twin matte black Glock 18s, one in each red-nailed hand.

The tenants of the Poseidon Motel ran from their respective rooms like chickens with their heads cut off, some of them butt naked and very ugly. The duo ignored the civilians.

"Nera, anything?" Afro said into a radio headset.

"He made me," came the reply. "I'm heading outside."

The sound of gunfire erupted again. There were several more exchanges of shooting followed by silence.

The two women in front started to circle around back.

"Nera, Nera, come in," the sistah with the afro said into her radio. No reply.

"See, Monique," blondie, who also had on a headset, said to the woman with the big 'fro. "I told you Marley is one treacherous motherfuckah." In contrast to her naughty school girl look, homegirl affected a straight-outta-Compton dialect.

4:24pm

"He's not Spider-Man, LaNetta. He can't climb walls, and he can't hold his breath longer than any other fool," Monique countered. "Well, not *much* longer."

"Shit," the blonde responded, moving cautiously forward. "You of all people know that niggah ain't been in the game this long 'cause marks catch him slippin'."

"Search and destroy, LaNetta," Monique answered,

moving forward herself. "That's what we do, and that's what Twelvetrees is paying us to get done."

The two went around back. There was a pool. In it, a woman in a velvet mini floated on her back in the reddening water. She was East Indian and had an intricate vine

tattoo covering one side of her face.

Marley's bullet had made a neat hole in the center of her head, ruining the artwork. Her lungs had filled with water, and the body began to slip slowly beneath the surface.

"Damn, he capped Nera," Monique said.

LaNetta snorted. "And he liked her—they used to fuck."

From the roof of the motel, where he'd clambered easily after the shooting started, Marley popped up and sprayed bullets at the two.

"Goddammit, he's got Nera's Ingram." LaNetta dove behind a Dumpster. Monique joined her.

Clinging flat to the roof again, Marley rolled for protection as their return fire sunk into the upper sections of the building.

"You see him?" Monique peeked from around the garbage bin.

"Naw," LaNetta answered, also looking up at the roof line.

The screech of sirens singed the air.

"We gotta get gone," LaNetta said. "We can't get into a shoot out with the po-po. Too much attention."

"Always slippery." Monique's good eye went stone.

"We'll get him, girlfriend." LaNetta touched her comrade's arm. "We'll get him for Nera." They booked.

Up on the roof, Marley could see the swirling carousel of red-and-blue lights approaching in the dark. He wiped his prints off the Ingram and dumped the piece in an air

duct. Quickly, he climbed off the roof and ran to where he'd stashed Guzmán.

"Who in the hell were those *locas?*" she asked.

Marley helped her out of the crawl space burrowed into the side of the motel. He'd put some crates in front of the entrance as camouflage.

"They call themselves the Furys."

"You sound like you know them."

"Yeah, worked a few jobs with those broads back in the day."

"Figures."

"This would be so much simpler if Saunders had provided you with an armed escort." The law got closer, and Marley hurried to retrieve his attaché case. He also brushed the dirt off his clothes.

"He said how I got there was my business. He told me he doesn't want to be seen giving a criminal like me the red carpet treatment."

Four cop cars swept into the courtyard.

"Opportunistic motherfuckah," Marley said, eyeing the cop cars.

"People have all kinds of reasons for doing what they do, Marley."

"Even you?"

4:36pm

"I'm just trying to survive."

The manager of the Poseidon Motel had been shot by one of the Furys. He was still alive, though the paramedics looked glum about his prospects. The police interviewed patrons of the motel trying to make sense of the chaos. Marley had decided it would draw too much attention if he and Guzmán tried to get away before the uniforms were through. People had been too busy covering their asses to ID him as the gunman on the roof.

"It was, like, these fine babes who were, like, deadly, dude," a surfer recounted to a dubious uniformed cop. "Like, whoa, man, you'd give serious attention to any one of 'em if you saw 'em at the club, but, like, man, I wouldn't want to piss any one of 'em off."

A female cop questioned Marley and Guzmán near the pool. "You two are on your way to San Diego, Mr. Goines?"

"That's right, sergeant," Marley answered. "My wife has business there with her marketing firm, and I had time off, so," he put an arm around Guzmán's shoulders and pulled her close, "we combined business and pleasure."

Guzmán planted a big wet smack on Marley's cheek. "I can't get enough of this guy." She smiled at the cop like a love-struck teenybopper.

The sergeant suppressed a sardonic grin and returned the well-made false drivers license Marley had given her. "And you've never seen these wild women before, I take it?"

"Oh my Lord, no," Guzmán gushed. "You'd certainly remember crazy *chicas* like them, huh, honey?"

"That's right," Marley said, bobbing his head up and down like a square.

The coroner's crew was pulling Nera out of the pool and putting her corpse into a body bag. Marley pretended like it bothered him. "Can we go, officer?"

The cop closed her notepad, clicking the plunger end

of her ballpoint against the cover. "Well, we have descriptions from the other customers." She regarded Marley for a second, but whatever question she was forming, she let it go. "Thanks for your time, folks."

"Our pleasure," Guzmán said, putting an arm around Marley's waist.

They had to hang around for another hour and a half as the authorities—some flew up via helicopter from San Diego—went over the crime scene. It seemed the cops' theory was the three had been after a Mr. Stark.

That was the name Marley had used on the registration card when he'd paid cash for the room. He hadn't listed Guzmán. But with the manager still in surgery, any description of the enigmatic Mr. Stark would be obtained later.

And because Carlsbad depended on tourism, some city bureaucrats showed up and comped the shook-up patrons to rooms elsewhere. Marley and Guzmán were deposited at a Triple-A-approved place not too many blocks away. There they showered, separately.

Thereafter, Marley stole a car from the parking lot. He drove further north toward a location where he kept a cache of supplies, a place few would suspect he used. He knew it was going to be a long night.

5:00pm

*   *   *

Samson Twelvetrees threw his Nokia cell phone against the wall of his office, shattering it. "Goddamn! Is this motherfucker David Blaine?"

"You mean the rap group?" Dee-Ray wondered. He leaned against the wall near his boss, working a toothpick among his crunchers. The 4XL-sized Samoan was dressed casual in Fubu and unlaced Skechers. His arms were def muscle and various Maori tattoos encircled his Hulk-sized arms.

Twelvetrees was going to pimp slap his goon but figured the boy didn't know any better. He composed himself, running his hands through his black hair swept back from his angular Indian face. He addressed Maurice, his right-hand man who sat in front of his desk, leafing through the latest issue of *Forbes*.

"Ideas?"

Maurice was a reedy, pasty-faced white boy from Kent in the U.K. with pinched features and limp hair. He affected an upper class English accent and favored mohair coats. Twelvetrees's right-hand man touched the side of his yellow-tinted Fossil glasses, thinking.

"There's a few possibilities, particularly this couple I

know. The price won't be cheap, but they'll get the job done." He paused, momentarily biting his bottom lip. "Mind you, they have their own way of doing things."

"As long as they get results. And what in the fuck do I care about price?" Twelvetrees stormed around his expensively appointed office. "I'm about to solidify my takeover of the biggest corporation in the drug world."

He stopped in front of an original Basquiat, his arms spread wide. "Get whoever it is, and get them on the payroll. I want to personally supervise this time in the field."

Maurice stood, adjusting his mohair coat. "I'm on it." He strode out of the office.

"And you," Twelvetrees said, pointing at Dee-Ray. "Get

your pork chop eatin' ass on the street and work our snitches. Between the border and Sacramento we've got hundreds of people in our network—housewives, architects, students, cops, judges, whoever and whatever. I've got some ballers right now riding up and down the rails in case they board a train. Somebody knows something. Find out where those two are and where they're heading."

"Cool, cool, it's done, Samson." The bruiser went into motion and left the office.

Twelvetrees checked his Bulova and sat down. He thumbed the flat widescreen on the wall near his desk to life via a built-in console. Right on schedule, California Attorney General Dakin Saunders was holding a live press conference broadcast on CNN. The A.G. wore a Brooks Brothers blue serge suit, white shirt, and red and

blue tie. Flanked by his flunkies, he stood before reporters and their electronic transmission engines.

5:30pm

In the background, men and women with the logos of DEA or Sheriff's Department stenciled on the back of their windbreakers were handcuffing some well-dressed people in front of a Century City office building.

"... behind me," Saunders was saying, "you see the results of Operation Zero Tolerance. This is my measure to bust not the low-level dealer, but the lawyers and bankers who launder the large sums of narco monies flowing through areas such as here, in Los Angeles. And I can assure you, these brigands won't be getting off with a slap on the wrist or plea bargaining their sentences." The camera pulled in tight on cue. "I will make sure harsh punishment is meted out for the crimes they have committed."

Twelvetrees stifled a yawn. His intercom buzzed, and his secretary announced his next appointment. In came Charise, a leggy Afro-Brazilian in DKNY bell bottoms and a straining stretch top. He undid his zipper.

On the screen, Saunders's big digital head turned as the disembodied voice of a reporter asked him a question. "Attorney General, is there any truth to the rumor that you've made a deal with Lina Guzmán, a leader in the drug trade?"

Saunders gave a politician's cobra smile. "That's news to me. But if any wrongdoer suddenly gets an attack of conscience, who am I to not at least listen to them?"

Charise peeled off her top. Then she gripped one of her healthy breasts and licked the nipple with an unusually long tongue. Twelvetrees got hard, and she got down to business between his spread legs. As Saunders droned on about how great a governor he was going to be, Charise's bobbing head cast a shadow on the TV images.

5:35pm

SAN JUAN
CAPISTRANO

It was funny as hell to Marley that Lina Guzmán was nervous around religious artifacts.

"You afraid you gonna get scorched by a lightning bolt?"

In his world, bullets and backstabbers killed you, not the unseen. He removed the map he'd been studying from the wall and set it afire on the stone floor of the St. Sebastian monastery.

"Shut up." She looked up nervously at the rough hewn silver cross tacked over an archway and moved off.

He hunched his shoulders and slipped his RP55 windbreaker over the Kani turtleneck and Phat Farm black jeans. He relocked the ornately carved 17th century oak armoire from which he'd retrieved these and several other items. He put his new "tools" in the Dunhill attaché case. He tossed his client a windbreaker in her size to go with the other attire he'd supplied her.

"I didn't ask for this, Marley. I didn't ask for Samson Twelvetrees to assassinate my father and get all this bullshit dumped on me."

"You mean you were content to enjoy your daddy's money while sippin' and swayin' at cocktail parties all over the world."

She put on the jacket. "Can we go?"

"Yes, ma'am."

They left the room and walked along an open air causeway.

"You don't know what it's like," she went on. "You operate alone. But be me and see if you can get respect from men who are used to only having women around to suck their cocks or hide packets of cocaine in their pussies."

"No one had your back, so you made the deal with Saunders to get out from under."

"As you would say, you Goddamn right I did." She stepped closer to him. "Look, Marley, I've used profits from the last two years to build health *clínicas*, invest in legal businesses, sponsor academic scholarships—"

He held up a hand. "That's why it was easy for Twelve-trees to turn your operation against you. You were fuckin' with their bank while gettin' your guilt stroked."

"I wanted to change things," she said. "I was out to make this a legit enterprise."

They walked in silence, then she stopped and said, "Admit it, Marley, I'm not the scummy self-centered be-yatch you assumed I was."

10:29pm

"None of us is all good or bad."

They stared at each other for several moments. The excitement of the past few hours and saving each other's lives had gotten under their skins. They drew closer ...

A cough sounded at the end of the causeway. "You all set, Mr. Pelecanos?"

"Yes, thank you." *And for not letting me get my swerve on.* "We'll be going."

Guzmán avoided eye contact with the park service ranger as the two walked past the woman. The St.

Sebastian Monastery, like several other historic mission landmarks in San Juan Capistrano, was overseen by the state. The night air was balmy, and the smell of jacaranda and jasmine was in full effect. Not too far away a train rumbled by.

They got to a parking structure near the train station. Once inside, Marley led the way to a recent model green and black Cadillac Eldorado with gold wire rims. They left in the car.

"How many of these kind of stashes do you maintain?" She wondered aloud. "Clothes, cars, weapons, that shit adds up."

"Sure do." No sense elaborating about the hideaway cribs and equipment he kept in various spots throughout the country—and elsewhere.

"Next stop L.A.?" she asked, still trying to get him to open up.

"Not directly."

"Fine," she said, giving up. He was in that zone of his.

The El-D got up on the highway, and Marley kept the car stoking at an even 85 m.p.h.

"What's the hurry?" Guzmán's brow wrinkled.

"We got a train to catch."

She hadn't noticed it, but they were on a part of the freeway running parallel to the tracks. The Caddy swooped past the passenger train that had recently departed the San Juan Capistrano depot. The car ate up asphalt, and soon they arrived at a station stop in

Mission Viejo. The joint had one outside bench and two broke-ass palm trees leaning next to it. No people were around except a sleepy clerk in a dimly lit booth. Marley bought tickets.

In less than a minute, the train belched into the station. The two boarded.

"This way." Marley walked toward another car, and Guzmán followed him. The car they entered was less populated, and he got them a seat about midway.

"Z'up?" She crossed her shapely legs, her dark eyes taking him all in.

"Wanted to smoke out whoever else might be on our ass. I spotted a tail on the road when we left San Juan Capistrano. I lost 'em." He tucked the attaché case beneath the seat.

"But who could have …" Guzmán began. "The park ranger in the monastery."

11:38pm

Marley nodded. "I guess if I can bribe 'em, someone else can bribe 'em better. She must have followed us and saw which car we took."

"I thought you never slipped." She rubbed a hand on his knee. "Or are you thinking about something other than business?"

He weighed his response, lost in the inviting black of her eyes. The door to the car opened, and he shifted his gaze to see who it was. The buster wasn't even trying to pretend he was something other than what he was. The hitter was polished mahogany and lethal, dap in a Prada suit complemented by steel-rimmed shades. The man had just clicked his cell phone off. No doubt he'd alerted Twelvetrees to their whereabouts.

"Fuck," Guzmán whispered, looking around. There was a woman, her two children, and a sleeping old man in the car too. But she knew the killer didn't care how many innocents he took out.

The door at the other end opened, and two more shooters, clean in their gear and projecting trouble, joined the party. Each was built like they could play D on the line for the Rams.

Marley had picked the seats they were in for a reason. He swiftly fished out his gat and took aim.

"Yo, niggah's fillin' his hand," Steel Rims hollered, reaching for his own cannon.

Marley shot the circuit box directly across from Guzmán and him. A fireworks of sparks spewed from the thing as the car's lights went black. The train was going through open land, a modicum of light pouring through the windows.

"Motherfuck," one of the other busters said, bumping into a seat.

"Oh my God, what's happening!" the woman with the children screamed. One of the kids started wailing.

"Stay on point," Steel Rims warned.

Several rounds of silenced fire ricocheted inside the car. The jacked shells rang hollow on the floor. The mother kept screaming, mingled with the crying of her children.

"Shut those brats the fuck up, bitch," Steel Rims ordered. "Or so help me all y'all's gonna get served." He drew toward the sound of the sniffling.

Marley had pushed Guzmán down on the floor and was crouched in the aisle with his night vision goggles on. He was worried most about Steel Rims, the obvious pro.

Marley kept his piece trained on the thug who'd bumped into the seat. A squeeze, a pop, and the top of the chump's head disappeared in a vermilion cloud. Some of the blood spattered on his partner.

Steel Rims was in motion. He grabbed one of the panicked children and hunkered behind him, using the kid as a shield. The other man stumbled for cover in the dark as Marley banged off a shot, missing him.

"Yo, Marley," Steel Rims said. "You better give us the queen, or this snot nose don't see no more birthdays." He twisted the child's arm to prove he wasn't playing.

"Let my son go," the woman pleaded, feeling for the baller. One of her hands brushed against him.

"Back the fuck up, moms." He backhanded the woman, knocking her away. Steel Rims had a gun pressed to the sobbing youngster's temple.

Marley could see all this with his goggles as he crept forward. The man behind him was also fumbling around.

"Marley, you've got to save that child," Guzmán implored him.

"Quiet," Marley said, but it was too late. The other man jumped her by locating the sound of her voice.

"Yeah, baby, I don't mind wrasslin' witchu," he slobbered.

Marley turned to help her, but Steel Rims was restless.

"I bet you can see me, huh? Well, let me hear you slide your gun to me, Marley, or I let some hollow points in junior."

11:49pm

"Please, mister, whoever you are, don't let him kill my baby," the mother begged.

Marley did as he was ordered.

"Now come over here and hand me them night specs or whatevah you got." Steel Rims stood still, holding onto the child.

The train rocked along the tracks.

"Come on, playah, don't be shy now."

"I got the ho," the other goon said, feeling up Guzmán. "Goddamn, her titties are bouncier than Jenny Lo-Lo's." He laughed as she fought against his hold.

"I'm waiting, Marley," Steel Rims said.

"I'm coming, bitch." Marley walked to the man and took off the goggles, letting them touch the dude's hand. "Let the boy go."

Steel Rims snatched the goggles and put them on. He still had an arm around the boy's throat, his gun held in the other hand.

"Fuck! You's a clever motherfuckah, ain't you?" He looked directly at Marley, smiling. "Now listen while I snap this little boy's neck 'fore I whack your ass."

"Naw, son." In a whirl of motion, Marley embedded one of the gaffs he'd taken off the knife man in TJ in the right lens of the goggles.

"You bitch!" Steel Rims blared in pain. He dropped his iron and groped for his face. Marley finished him with a kick to the torso, then a hammer blow to his temple.

"Yo, what the fuck just went down up in this muh fuh," the last shooter demanded. "I better hear some squawkin' or this chickenhead is gonna have a broke neck."

Marley breathed shallowly as he'd been taught in covert training. *Be like a motherfuckin' ninja*, they'd drilled into him over and over. *Be one with your environment.* Silently, he went back to where the two stood, imagining he was walking on leaves so he'd tread as lightly as possible. Behind him, the woman and children whimpered.

"Look here, I ain't bullshittin'," the assassin repeated. He put a headlock on Guzmán. "Tell him, girl."

"Take him, Marley," she rasped.

"Wrong answer, trick." He tightened his grip, and with

his other hand, began letting off shots. His bullets ping-pinged everywhere.

"What up now, huh hero?" he hollered, blindly trying to pinpoint Marley.

Guzmán stamped on the last man's foot and shoved.

They both tumbled backwards.

"That's your ass, ho," the man promised. He brought his gun up to pistol whip her. Marley gambled and leaped from where he'd gone flat on the floor. He collided with their bodies, and they all rolled around. The gun went flying.

The two men got to their feet and traded blows like Holyfield and Lewis in the gloom, huffing and grunting. Marley executed a drop kick, upending the bigger man on his backside. Pouncing, Marley got his hands around the man's neck. He slammed the fool's box of a head into the floor several times until the punk was still.

Marley rose, helping Guzmán get to her feet. Suddenly the lights came back on.

11:53pm

"Back up power," he gulped, his mouth hanging open from exertion. He scooped up his gat and retrieved the briefcase. Through the glass in the door leading to the front of the train, he saw the engineer and conductor running toward their car. The conductor was carrying a club.

"We better jet," Marley said. "I can deal with them, but no doubt they already buzzed the cops."

As one, the pair went in the other direction. The woman and her children were huddled in their seats. The old man sat up, his mouth hanging open, blinking in shock.

Marley and Guzmán got in the tiny passageway between the cars. She hefted the attaché case. He got the platform door open with a precise kick. Outside in the cold night, the landscape went whipping by.

"Are you joking?" She stared at him.

"Hell no."

He blew a hole through the glass to stop the two coming for them. The train slowed as it went into a bend. He'd reached into the case, snapped it shut, and tossed it away from the train. Then he pulled her to him as he leapt onto a slope dropping away from the tracks. Marley wrapped himself around her, controlling her fall so she wouldn't break any bones. A black helicopter arched over the train through the starless night.

The pair rolled and wound up in a clump of weeds. Marley was on top of her, each breathing hard.

The woman said in his ear, "You're something, you know that, Marley?" She started to get her grind on.

But the overhead whoosh of the chopper's blades got them up and running like a modern version of Poitier and Curtis in *The Defiant Ones*.

11:58pm

12:07am
Somewhere in the Night

They sprinted down the embankment. Overhead, the helicopter shot past them.

"Maybe they're not after us," Guzmán said.

Marley snorted. He indicated a culvert and, once there, dove into a clump of shrubbery lining the trench. The 'copter circled back. Marley's face was a frozen mask as he looked through the shrubs, watching the thing.

"They're waiting for a clear shot. It's not mounted with a fifty-caliber, so we might have a chance."

"What a comfort."

"You want to live?"

"You know the answer to that."

"Good. Follow my orders and follow me." He got up and trotted along the culvert, Guzmán close behind him. She was in shape. Several shots echoed behind them and she stumbled.

He turned and got a hold of her arm. "Don't think, just do."

She was on her feet as their pursuers swung back

around. Marley bounded out of the culvert, and she did the same. They were speeding across open ground, and she knew at any second both of them could be cut down.

Abruptly, he pushed her flat. Marley pivoted around in a crouch as the craft zeroed in on the pair. A figure leaned out of its cargo door, a weapon blazing tracer fire.

Guzmán covered her head, fighting panic as bullets tore chunks out of the ground not more than five yards from them.

"I got something for you, asshole."

From his coat pocket he'd removed one of the small metallic disks he'd removed from the Dunhill case. Gunfire whizzed past Marley's head as he threw it expertly, and it magnetically clamped onto the underside of the craft, beneath the cockpit. The device exploded, and smoke filled the chopper. The attackers veered off.

"Come on."

They made it into a stand of poplars, and he halted their escape. He sniffed the air.

"You part wolf?" she only half-joked.

"Open fires, charred meat and fish ... campgrounds not too far away. We'll stay in this wooded area while we head over there." He pointed in the direction he meant.

12:11am

"I guess if we run into a bear, you can take him too, huh?"

He started to jog away, and she kept up. Soon they reached the edge of the small woods. Sure enough, they'd come upon a camping area replete with tents, fishing poles, and smoldering fires. There were two RVs and several regular passenger vehicles parked as well.

"Which one?" she asked.

"That Marquis wagon—it's the closest to us. I don't want to raise no ruckus if I don't have to."

Marley and Guzmán crept forward to the car. As he'd hoped, the door was unlocked, and Marley eased in and got busy with his pen knife beneath the dash. Guzmán had her arms folded, watching him with a smile on her face.

"Hey, you." A middle-aged man in shorts and slippers emerged from some greenery opposite the way they'd come. He was zipping up his fly.

"Mister," Marley began, having already straightened up.

"That's your ass, buddy." The man shook a finger at him as he advanced.

"William?" a female voice said from within the nearby tent.

Guzmán raised her Beretta above her head and put two in the air, disturbing the birds in the branches. "Back the fuck up."

William halted immediately.

The woman stuck her head out. "What the—"

"Shhh," Guzmán put a finger across her lips, glaring at the woman.

Marley got the car started. "We've worn out our welcome."

They got in and took off. The couple stood in the roadway, looking at their car get farther and farther away. Other campers started appearing.

"You got style, Lina."

"I like it when you say my name."

To her surprise, he smiled. They drove on.

The car eventually jostled along an unpaved, rutted path. The undercarriage creaked, and their heads bounced against the headliner. Marley attempted to balance speed with handling as he drove the old station wagon into the mountains. He came to a turn-off. Momentarily he hesitated on which way to go. There was a whoosh from overhead. The black helicopter was back.

Guzmán said, "I'd hoped they were through."

"We just bought some time, that's all. That's a modified Bell 407 with armor plating. They set down and patched it up. Probably near the camp, and either their guns or, more likely, some dead presidents got them the information about what kind of car we'd be in."

"How come that thing is so quiet now?" Guzmán watched it glide past then bank into a turn.

"Whisper mode." Marley was already heading down one of the roads. This one in worse shape than the one they'd just been on. He plowed ahead. The steering wheel suddenly wrenched from his control, and he had to grab it quick, lest they slam into a boulder or roll the car. Soon there was a loud snap, and the left side of the car listed badly.

12:26am

"Shit," Marley said, "part of the A-frame's given way."

"Can we still go?"

The grinding of the wheel in the tire well provided the answer. "The sidewall can't take this for long," he said. As predicted, they got another twenty yards when the tire unraveled in an explosion of compressed air. Strips of rubber flew past the driver's window as Marley kept driving on the metal rim. The front end on the car sunk to a stop in the road, and the two piled out.

"Where are we?" She started running toward a dense knot of looming trees.

"Don't know exactly. What matters is we get to ground we can protect."

They got to the trees as the helicopter swooped at them. Marley expected gunfire and tackled Guzmán, bringing her down. They landed on a bed of leaves.

"I don't believe we have time for romance right now, baby." But she did grind on him.

They got up and ran again, moving as best they could through the gloom. The helicopter maintained its presence overhead, an alloy-and-glass vulture. The two emerged from the forest.

"Look down there." Guzmán stopped, catching her breath.

In the valley below was a series of one- and two-story buildings of mismatched design. There was a water tower at the end of the one main street, bifurcating the cluster of buildings. The evidence of long disuse showed from the amount of broken windows and general dreariness that engulfed the hamlet.

"In there," Marley said.

They descended toward a squarish two-story structure with a dome roof. Inset along the sides of the building on the second floor were large cathedral windows.

The helicopter went into a hovering position near the water tower. The duo gained the side of the building, and Marley peered around the corner. "What the hell ...?" he muttered. A large billowing shape emerged from the helicopter, balancing itself on the landing skid of the aircraft.

The shadowy figure leaped from the skid to the water tower, a long coat or cape whipping about the figure. Another similar shape remained balanced on the skid. This second apparition also jumped onto the circular observation deck of the water tower.

"Whatever," Marley said. He got a door to the building open, and they went inside. Their footsteps rang hollow on the concrete floor.

"This must have been some kind of manufacturing plant," Guzmán said, touching various large, indistinct objects in the room.

Marley pushed a heavy steel desk in front of the door. "I think this was some sort of electrical power plant. Those things you were touching are turbines."

"Are we going to be safe here?" She came over to help him as he lifted a second desk into place.

"We're not safe anywhere. But we'll survive." From the inner pockets of his coat he took out a Sig Sauer P226 and handed it to her. "I removed a few items from my attaché case before we jumped from the train, just in case we got separated from it. This bad rascal has better stopping power than your Beretta."

"Prepared for everything ain't you? The big papa boy scout."

"Shit."

"So now what?"

"We keep moving. If we stay in this building, we're dead meat. I just needed a moment to get our shit together."

"Okay?"

He pointed toward the ceiling. "Do the unexpected."

Guzmán clambered up a ladder to a catwalk ahead of him. Once there, Marley looked out one of the large windows at the water tower.

"The chopper's coming this way. There must be a trap door to the roof."

"Over here," Guzmán said. She was already ascending a set of iron rungs built into the wall.

The Bell's rotors could be heard beating the air outside the building. "Hurry," Marley bellowed. He tapped her on the butt.

"Harder, honey, harder," she laughed. "Hold on."

12:33am

Guzmán took aim at a padlock on the hatch to the roof.

"Hey, that bullet could ricochet and clip us," Marley said. He reached past her and using a slim blade from his Swiss Army knife, quickly got the cheap lock open. They scrambled outside. The sleek Bell Jetcopter was hovering near the building. The thing looked formidable, the moonlight shining on its black sheen. From the cargo door on the side, a man looked out.

"Samson," Guzmán gasped.

Samson Twelvetrees's face was partially visible in the

dark gap of the doorway. He waved at her as if saying goodbye to an old friend. Blackness overlapped his features as he stepped back. Then something glinted in the maw of the ship.

Guzmán slipped, nearly tumbling off the rounded roof as they headed toward its apex.

"I've got you!" Marley yelled and grabbed her arm. Together, each supporting the other, they crab-crawled upwards. There was a whoosh from behind them. Glass broke, and an explosion ripped through the building. Marley and Guzmán had made the peak of the arch. A pyramid of flame suddenly geysered through one side of the dome, nearly roasting the woman. The wave of heat and concussive force knocked Marley down, and he had to dig his fingers into the roof tiles to keep from falling away.

"Bazooka," was his terse explanation as she helped him get up.

Another shell tore into the roof, not far from where they were. The building shook as the second round went off. The two slid on their backsides down the curvature to its edge, where a thick ledge allowed them a moment's footing.

"Oh fuck," she said.

"Oh yes," he said.

He gave her a nudge, and the two leapt from the roof.

They came down on the one-story building next door. Marley twisted around, pointing his piece.

The helicopter floated above the domed building as flames blistered the cathedral windows. The remaining panes popped as the heat intensified. The craft tilted upward. Marley and Guzmán extended their guns. The helicopter came forward, then veered off. It rose in the air and flew away.

12:39am

"Seems like they want to herd the rabbits." Marley was already exploring the roof for a way down. The building was made of brick, the flat roof covered in loose shingles.

They went down an ancient, shaky gutter attached to the side of the building to the dirt street. The building next door was on fire from within, casting a pulsating light in several directions.

"Something's really whack about this place." Marley frowned as the fire weirdly lit their surroundings. "This damned building looks like a bank outta some *Bonanza* rerun. And this one," he pointed, "is out of pictures I've seen of Chicago in the thirties."

"We can take in the architecture later. Right now we have to stay alive." Guzmán yanked on his arm.

"Sure you right. Come on, 'round this corner out of the light."

With him leading the way, they went down a narrow passageway between the buildings. A billowing night creature dropped down from above in front of them.

"What is that, Marley?" She'd pushed against his back, and he could feel the rhythm of her heart doing double time.

Marley shot at it. The creature suddenly lifted off the ground and disappeared into the dark sky, laughing a very human laugh as it did so.

"Oh, Jesus." Guzmán's mouth flew open.

Marley set his jaw, and they ran the rest of the way down the passageway. At the end, the pair took a left. Marley strained to hear footsteps along the rooftop overhead but discerned no movement. They came to a stop alongside what appeared to have been a boxing arena. They rested against a wall.

"Marley, what the fuck was that thing back there?"

"A man that can be killed," he said.

"I hope you're right."

"Don't start getting all native and superstitious on me, girl."

They walked toward the rear, a ring with sagging ropes and worn out punching bags dangling from the ceiling like prehistoric cocoons.

"Marley," a voice called out.

The two stood still.

"Marley." The voice had a hollow, discordant effect, as if it were coming to them through a long tube. "Marley and Lina Guzmán, we have come for you, and there is no respite."

Up on the edge of the roof of the burning power plant a figure stood, black and one dimensional against the bright yellow background of flame. Its arms were spread wide, and the ends of a cloak flapped in the wind. Marley wasn't sure, but it seemed as if red slits gleamed where the eye sockets should be.

"Damn," Guzmán said hoarsely.

"Bullshit." Marley squeezed off three rounds at the mysterious figure. The man went over backward, swallowed by the fire. "So much for that punk ass Freddy Krueger," he said.

They went around the building, their guns out and ready. At the corner they stopped again, listening.

Guzmán asked, "How are we going to get out of here?"

"The helicopter, when it comes back."

Guzmán went pale at the prospect of being transported in the air.

Marley felt assured, confident once more. He stepped into an open area next to the building. The idea that the fake phantom act was supposed to unnerve him made him angry. What the hell kind of shit was that? Like he was supposed to be some jittery teenager getting all worked over—

12:46am

A flash of claws swept over his face.

"Arghh!" He grabbed at his cheek, falling to the dirt.

"Marley!" Guzmán screamed.

Blood was on his fingertips, but he had no time to dwell on his wound as another talon came at his face. He drew back, blasting away with his pistol. The gun had no effect.

"Fuck." Guzmán blazed away too.

The nether being in front of him jumped and cavorted as Marley lay on the ground, watching the wraith dance. Guzmán stood nearby, her gun also pointed at the creature.

Marley got on his feet. The fire bursting from the power plant threw elongated shadows all over the place. The thing moved in and out of the light, taunting him. Marley shot at the head this time.

"Ow, that stings." The man-bat stopped prancing and stood still. It was a woman, at least six-two, decked in some kind of stretch attire that covered her body from the neck down. A cape was attached at her shoulders with loops of cloth connected to her wrists. She wore shiny black stomping boots.

What really stood out was her bleached white face and heavily mascaraed eyes that contrasted her red orbs. Her fanged canines completed the package.

Marley shot at her head again. A black smudge appeared on her forehead, and she wiped it away.

He threw the gun aside, disgusted. Marley and the tall

woman circled each other like wrestlers. She sprang at him. He let her weight take him down, then flipped her over onto her back. Wasting no time, he got to his feet, whipping kicks at her head. But the woman was fast and scuttled out of the way.

Guzmán shot at her, but like before, the bullets did nothing.

"Blanks," Marley said. "It's all part of the freak show."

"Is it, Marley?" The other shadow, the man he'd shot at on the roof, stood at the periphery of the clearing, arms outstretched. He let his arms down and strode forward. He was dressed more conservatively in a black, double-breasted Calvin Klein suit and matching collarless shirt. He also had a cape flowing from his shoulders, but not attached to his wrists like his partner's. His face was a duplicate of the woman's—including the fangs and glowing eyes.

"Your little 99 Cent Store Christopher Lee act supposed to make me shit on myself?" The expediter stood ready in the center of the open space.

"Quite," the man replied. He was tall, six-five Marley guessed, and there was a hypnotic quality to his deep voice. He came closer. He smelled of dead earth.

Marley spun around and lashed a leg out at the woman. He caught her full in the abdomen, and her body bent forward in pain. A tight, satisfied smile creased his face. "Y'all can be hurt."

The woman back-flipped twice to the edge of the light.

She watched them, her lupine eyes shiny with glee. The man walked to her, avoiding getting close to Marley. He'd produced twin World War II-era Thompson submachine guns.

12:49am

"What have we gotten into?" Guzmán sighed, pressed back-to-back to Marley.

"Can you feel the fear, Marley?" the man said. He handed one of the machine guns to the woman. Cheerfully, she slid the weapon's firing bolt into place. The burning timbers in the power plant crackled loudly.

"We're dead."

"Not until they've had their fun," Marley said.

The man and woman fanned out, striding at ninety degree angles to each other—the perfect cross fire to cut their targets to pieces.

"I asked you, Marley," the man repeated, "do you feel the fear?"

Through clamped teeth he said, "Bring it on."

Guzmán gripped his arm, the anticipation of death pulling the skin tight across her brown face.

The man barked off a few rounds from the Thompson, the bullets burying themselves inches from Marley's feet. He didn't flinch.

"Goddammit," Guzmán swore, sagging on weak knees.

The fanged woman laughed lustfully. "Beg, Marley. Beg like the big, black, ferocious dog you are."

She raked off some of her clip at his head, causing him to duck. She lowered the gun toward the middle of his body. She ran her tongue over her fangs.

The man-and-woman goth hit team gazed lovingly at each other. As if they were sharing a telepathic thought, both gleamed hellish smiles at Marley and Guzmán.

"This is too easy, too quick," the woman said. "We want it to be sport, to be exciting." She rubbed her hand on her partner's crotch.

"You mean you want to get off," Marley said.

"That too, handsome," she admitted. Her hand rubbed her man's area some more.

"This is classic, is it not, Marley? The hunters and the hunted," the man proclaimed.

"What if we don't run?" Guzmán said. "What if we don't let you sick motherfuckahs have your fun? You're going to kill us anyway. Get it done like Marley said."

"Ask your boyfriend," the fanged woman countered.

Marley was already moving, tugging on Guzmán to follow.

She jerked her hand away. "No," she said. "I'm tired, Marley. Tired of all this bullshit."

Marley could see the man and woman were delighted to hear her defeat. It fed their baroque sense of torture.

Guzmán's shoulders sagged. "This has become all so pointless."

He put her upper arms in a lock with his hands. "Lina, as long as we're breathing there's a chance."

"Marley, I . . ."

"Yes, Lina?" the fanged woman taunted.

The expediter took her hand. They gazed at each other.

"We're getting bored," the man said. "You get a minute head start." He let off another burst as Marley and Guzmán ran into the trees.

"I'm wet," the woman told her man, stroking her machine gun.

1:00am

1:03am
Cleveland National Forest, Riverside County

Marley wasn't down with being the goat—especially for these sick fucks. He was also pissed at himself for acting like a mark in San Juan Capistrano. But if he got out of this, he'd deal with that too.

"Which way?" Guzmán ran beside him.

"We have to keep doing the opposite of what they're expecting."

"Which is?"

"We're gonna jump 'em."

"Maybe that running around in the heat earlier has affected you, son. I've got three shots left in my Beretta, and our other guns are useless. And you don't have your attaché case."

"I have this." He showed her the grenade he'd put in his jacket pocket. "They're so sure of themselves, they didn't bother to search us."

"When we jumped from the train, you had that?"

"Bet."

"We could've been blown to—" She stopped herself and merely shook her head. "One grenade doesn't exactly balance the scale. Plus," she tapped the casing, "how do you know this wasn't fooled around with too?"

He jiggled it slightly in his palm. "This was with us from the Charger, not the monastery. What I figure is we circle back to the town."

"Why?" she asked. They began moving again, following a stream.

"A fundamental principle is never to remain completely passive, but to attack the enemy frontally and from the flanks, even while he is attacking us."

"Sun Tzu?"

"Von Clausewitz, baby. These punks are really into their thing. They want us to be scared."

He got silent, his anger cold, a straight razor chilled in ice water. Marley was not one for being on the defensive.

1:04am

"Lina," the woman's voice called from somewhere. "You know how bad Twelvetrees wants you, don't you? He said we could do whatever we wanted as long as we told him about it afterwards. And I have some yummy ideas with you tied spread eagle over a rock and my gun barrel I want to try out. Maybe we'll signal him back so he can watch."

Guzmán chewed her lip.

"Tune it out," Marley ordered. "She's just fucking with your head."

The two quit following the stream and went off into a section of trees and brush bunched together tightly. This prevented them from moving quickly, but they still moved ahead. Behind them, Marley could hear the rustle of foliage. They came to a wide thatch of thorny plants, cat's claw and huisache, as tall as they were. Their forward path was blocked.

Marley listened, his features keen with apprehension, as the sound he'd been listening for repeated itself. He hurled himself sideways, pulling on Guzmán as he fell. Machine gun fire made pulp of the stalks in front of them. The two crawled through the thicket. Marley had one arm up to try to ward off some of the scratches to their faces. Their clothes were torn, and numerous thorns became embedded in the material and their flesh.

"Marley," Guzmán cried out, "we can't make it, we can't even see where we're going."

"Quiet," he rasped.

The Thompson spat again, rounds like blind wasps buzzed in the air around them. The woman, as Marley knew, was using Guzmán's voice to locate them.

He kept going and Guzmán had no choice but to keep up.

He got to the edge and could feel smooth dirt as his hand groped the ground. The expediter got beside Guzmán.

"Don't move," he warned her, his lips on her ear.

"This is it, isn't it?" Her voice quavered, but she'd had presence of mind to speak softly.

"Don't move," he repeated. Crocodile-like, he slithered back through the thorns, each foot agonizing to plow through.

"Marley, I want to see the blood on your black skin," the fanged woman said.

Was the man playing possum? Marley wondered. Or more likely they'd split up to better their chances of running the two of them to ground. The digging and gouging of the thorns seemed endless, a special level of punishment reserved just for him. But he kept moving. Marley promised himself he wasn't going to die tonight.

The Thompson barked again, its bullets churning up vegetation and earth. "Scared of a twist, Marley?" the fanged woman taunted. She laughed, and her gun went off again. "You should be running through the jungle like your mama was calling for your monkey ass."

Marley stopped crawling. Blinking, he wiped blood and sweat from his face. As he'd hoped, he'd been able to use her gunfire to approximate her position in the inky foliage.

"I heard something, Marley." The fanged woman's silhouette was bent forward, the machine gun thrust before her.

Marley crept forward then stopped—intuition setting off his radar.

The Thompson sprayed, the bullets vipping into the dirt near him. He didn't move as the line of fire got closer, closer. A millimeter from him, with his arms drawn over his head, the firing halted. She wasn't sure where he was and wasn't going to waste her clip. But she wasn't going to call for help either, though her man would be coming, anxious to join in on the joy of slaughter.

1:16am

"I don't think I got you, did I, Marley? No, that would be too ordinary, and I will so enjoy slicing off your balls while I jack you off."

He could hear her getting closer to the section of plants where he concealed himself on his haunches.

"Fuck you." Marley sprang and hit her full on with a flying drop kick that sent her sprawling.

The fanged woman was up quickly, the machine gun cranking off shots once more. Her partner appeared. Marley made himself scarce.

"We have him now," the fanged man gloated.

"I'll get him."

"But—"

"I'll get him. You make sure his girlfriend doesn't run off. She's in that tangle of thorns over there." Marley's kick had knocked out one of her red lenses, and it gave her vampire look a grade B effect.

"Are you sure you don't want help?" Briefly his stage voice dropped and genuine concern shaded his words.

"I'll be back with the buck." She marched off.

Marley hadn't gone far. If he ran, she'd catch him and cut him down. His only opportunity to get the drop on

her was to stick close and take another chance on an attack. A tree branch poked in his back, and he smiled thinly. He got his Swiss Army knife out again and started working.

Determined, the fanged woman trod through the forest. She was going to prove that Marley wasn't going to make a fool of her twice. Despite her prey's obviously superior hand-to-hand combat skills, she knew he couldn't snatch bullets out of the air. She was excited.

Marley used the drawstring from his jacket and tied his hastily made bundle together. He was now hunkered behind a tree. For this to work he was going to have to show himself. His timing had to be perfect. He took some deep breaths, got psyched, then bolted.

The woman saw him and fired. Marley barely got to cover behind a rock formation. The bullets from the machine gun ate into the stone.

"No place else to hide, Marley."

She got closer.

"Show yourself and take it like a man. I know you're no punk."

Marley stepped from behind the rocks and threw his makeshift spear. She was firing as he did so. The spear was several hacked-off tree branches he'd carved points on and tied together. The crude weapon found its target and sunk into her upper thigh.

She hollered. Marley was on her, first making sure to knock the Thompson loose. The gun clattered out of her

grip. He caught her upside her head, and the woman crashed to the ground. Marley scrambled on top of her.

"Do I make you hard, Marley?" Her one red eye glared at him.

"When I kill you."

1:35am

They rolled, the spear snapping in two, the business end still embedded in her thigh. But she was going to finish this job herself; she wasn't about to yell for help. They slid to a stop along gravel, at the shore of a lake the stream flowed into.

The woman leveraged a pointy knee into his stomach.

Marley gasped and countered by getting his hands around her throat.

"Yes," she begged.

This threw him off, and she used his surprise to jab him in the kidneys. She'd somehow slipped on studded brass knuckles, and Marley buckled from the pain. She got loose and knocked him hard in the jaw with the knucks, stunning him. "This is going to be delightful."

Marley backed up, slipping and tumbling into the lake. She leapt on him, and they tussled in the bone-chilling water. Part of her makeup was coming off, and up close it made her appearance even more ghastly, like an experiment in humanity gone wrong. The flat of his hand chopped at her shoulder blade.

She answered with a blow to his jaw. Stars exploded behind his eyes, and Marley sunk beneath the murky water. Her steel-tipped nails scraped at his face. He pulled on her arms, bringing her under too.

The woman wrapped her legs around Marley's torso and squeezed. She had hard muscle under all her get-up, and air bubbles escaped from his lungs. Marley willed himself to be calm. Her hands reached for him again, clutching at his coat sleeve. He used this as a guide to find her, latching onto her cape that swirled about them. His lungs ached, and his reflexes slowed as energy and oxygen left his body.

Like a mountain climber clinging to one last rope, he drew the cape to him hand-over-hand. The woman realized what he was doing, and she stopped grabbing for him. She tried to undo the garment as Marley pressed against her, having found his way to her in the murk. He wound the cape around her throat and tightened. This time, being strangled didn't turn her on. Water rushed into her lungs.

Marley had to go slack because he was running out of air. He began to black out and had to let her go. They both broke the surface, gasping. He looked around, getting his bearings. The woman was swimming toward the shore, and, fortunately for Marley, her partner wasn't on the scene. Or at least he wasn't showing himself.

Marley stroked after her. In the near distance, he heard the Beretta shooting. If the fanged woman got to her gun, he'd be through. She was strong and fast, but her cape slowed her down. Yet if she halted to get it loose, it was certain Marley would be on her. The woman got out of the water and searched for her weapon. Behind her she could hear Marley's splashes getting closer. She spotted her Thompson and limped for it.

She was turning and firing as Marley dropped on her.

He knocked the wind out of her, and she staggered back, disoriented. A sharp crack of the side of his foot to the side of her head, and she dropped to her knees. Try as she might, it seemed impossible to get her chin off her chest. Slowly her head came up, and she stared blankly at the man looming before her. *The Thompson, get the Thompson up,* she told herself. Her arms couldn't obey the command.

"What's my name, bitch?"

"Fuck you," she replied. "Come here and kiss me." Blood dripped from her swollen mouth. She flicked her tongue and clacked her fake fangs.

"I'll pass." The heel of his shoe slammed into the bridge of her nose, and she went over and out. For insurance, he stepped over her and brought his foot down on her skull casing. He cared little whether she was breathing or not. Blood oozed from several wounds on her face, and her nose was bent sideways

Marley picked up the Thompson and went to look for her partner.

2:21am

Carefully, he picked his way back to the thorny plants. He stopped but could sense no movement, no presence nearby.

"Lina," he rasped, ducking should the man let go with a burst. There was no response, and a bad feeling tugged on his guts. "Lina," he called out, bolder this time. Again, only crickets and the croak of a frog.

Marley didn't relish another trip though the thorns, but what else could he do? The job was to get his client to her appointment with the conniving Saunders by three this afternoon. And he hadn't botched a job in all these years. She had to be alive, because Marley wasn't about half-steppin'.

There was a yelp of pain, and Marley had his answer: the fanged man had captured Lina. He hadn't killed her immediately in the off chance Marley had survived his encounter with his woman. That's why he hadn't come running, because the gunfire from the Beretta meant Lina

Guzmán had put up a fight, and that had kept him busy.
A cackle like a villain from an old movie on AMC echoed
through the cottonwoods.

Marley took the bait and stalked off in the direction of
the collection of mismatched buildings in the valley. He

came to the opposite end from the power plant. The
building was smoldering, the smell of burnt wood float-
ing everywhere. Marley looked around, deciding which
place the freak would have picked. He settled on a
steeple-like edifice piercing the sky. The place might or
might not be a church, but sure as anything, it would fit
in with the fuckhead's goth-vampire act.

He'd forgotten about the grenade and was pleased to
feel its heft inside his soaking windbreaker. He peeled off
the jacket, shivering in the warm night air. He couldn't
blow up the building with his client inside, so he put the
jacket with the grenade aside. The Thompson's magazine
felt light, and he guessed less than a fifth of the rounds
were left. There might have been another clip hidden on
the fanged woman's body, but another scream from Lina
Guzmán got him refocused.

"Beg for deliverance, cocaine queen!" the man hollered,
laughing with Vincent Price glee. "Give me Marley."

Naturally, they were in the top of the steeple. The part
of the building that faced the main street was set with
double doors. One door was slightly ajar.

"Come in, hero. We're waiting for you." He made
Guzmán scream again.

Marley went flat against the building, looking up. The goth hitman was leaning out over an open-air arch below the steeple.

"Come on, Marley. I don't want to get the party started without you."

"Kill him, Marley, kill this ghost-faced motherfuckah," Guzmán yelled.

Marley heard a smack. Guzmán groaned. He held himself back, knowing he couldn't completely play the monster's game. Carefully, Marley inserted the barrel of the Thompson in the crack between the doors. He pushed, opening the gap wider, wider ... until he felt tension. It was so slight he wasn't sure he hadn't imagined the sensation. *At times like this,* he reminded himself, *it was good to be paranoid.*

2:34am

* * *

"Marley?" The man leaned over the railing at the arch. He scanned the area with his infrared contacts. "Where did you go? Don't tell me you got scared and are going to leave your damsel to suffer more distress."

He looked over his shoulder at Guzmán. She was stripped to her panties, tied with metal cable to an inclined board of double weight plywood. He walked over to her.

"I want him to watch as I do you before we do him."
The fanged man took the pliers he'd found and gently,
teasingly gripped her already bleeding nipple.

"I hope he's blown the face off your ho." Guzmán spat
at him.

"You better hope he hasn't." He squeezed the pliers,
smiling.

Over her screams the fanged man heard a voice calling
out. "Shut up," he said, punching her again. The goth-
clad man let the pliers drop and ran back to the railing.
Guzmán was close to passing out. As the torturer leaned
over, there was an explosion. The floor vibrated and
smoke rose from the doorway where he'd rigged his
device. On the ground in front of the building lay
Marley, his body burnt and decimated. Portions of his
head were scattered about in bloody chunks.

Triumphantly, the fanged man turned and made for the
stairs, leaving his machine gun propped against the wall.
"I'll be right back, my darling," he said to Guzmán. "And
when I return, we'll get busy."

He reached the ground floor and rushed out of the
still-smoldering entranceway. He went over to the dead
body, bent down and rolled the corpse over. It was the
woman's body dressed in Marley's pants and shirt. Only
part of her head remained intact.

He was too stunned to wail.

Marley, clad solely in his Joe Boxers, said, "Your girl was
tough. I thought I'd broken her neck down at the stream.
But that tough heifer was alive and came stumbling back
here, dazed and fucked up." He paused, letting it build. "I
managed to get my clothes on her easily enough though."

"Then you aimed her toward the door."

"Yeah." Marley leveled the Thompson.

"I loved her," the other man said. He'd dropped his
vampire voice.

"Ain't that sweet."

The fanged man hurtled toward Marley, his cape

flapping behind him. The machine gun chattered. Bullets tore the man open with ragged holes as he wheeled to the earth, dead. Marley threw the Thompson down and stepped over to the body. He crouched down, searched the corpse. He noted a shoulder harness hidden beneath the folds of the cape. Then the chilled brother trotted into the building where Guzmán was.

"You bastard," Guzman said between blistered lips. She was listless, her eyes closed.

"It's me, Lina." Marley set about getting the cable loose, which cut into her skin.

She got a bleary eye open. "Timing your rescues a little close, huh, *hombre*?"

"Come on." He got the binding undone and scooped her up in his arms.

"I'm heavier than I look," she joked feebly.

"You're telling me." Marley carried her to a corner where there was some tarp. He laid her on it and went to find her clothes. When he returned with her garments, she was sitting propped against the wall.

3:03am

"Did you come back just for the balance of your money, Marley?" She stood and began to get dressed. Neither one took their eyes off the other as she did so.

"I'm a pro, remember? How would it be if I got away and didn't save you?"

"Protecting your reputation." She snuggled into her Versaces.

He pulled out a cell phone he'd scavenged from the dead man. "This was to call the helicopter and your boyfriend, Samson Twelvetrees, to come fetch the killers. The man had it on him. And the cable he tied you up with was part of the rig he used to do that flying bit in the alley."

"All part of the show," she said. Guzmán slipped on her DKNY shirt but didn't button it up. "So let me guess, you're going to try the redial button."

"Not exactly. I considered doing that, but what if

Twelvetrees shows up again with a chopper full of hoo-bangers?"

"Then you'd take care of business."

She pressed on him, her blouse open. "Before we get going again, I wanted to thank you properly." Her mouth was open as she kissed and tongued him. Marley held her tight.

He cupped one of her breasts through her lacy bra. He was careful not to go near her sore nipple. The expediter broke contact even as she slipped her hand through the slit of his boxers.

"Anyway, Ms. Guzmán," he said, kissing the tip of her nose. "I'm hoping this thing's roaming area will let me make a call to L.A."

"You're a tease."

He chuckled. "We do have a schedule to keep." He thumbed a number on the cell and it went through.

"Garvin, it's Marley," he began after the line connected, "I need a hook up." He talked some more on the phone making arrangements for what he needed next, then ended the call.

Marley said, "We have to get over to Santa Ana in Orange County."

She folded her arms, regarding him. "You going to walk around like that?"

"I'm on that, baby." He punched several buttons on the phone. "Write these down, will you? I'm going to get my pants."

Guzmán took the phone that now displayed its stored numbers. *Now where the hell was she going to get a pen?*

He went back outside and took the pants off the dead man. He'd purposely not shot him below the waist. For a shirt, he was going to be out of luck. He retrieved his shoes where he'd left them, next to his soaked wind-breaker. Wringing the jacket out, he went back in the building. Guzmán was already coming down the stairs, and together they exited the place for good.

Outside a fog had lumbered in. The two put their arms around each other for comfort. They walked past the dead bodies, not bothering to look at them.

As they hiked along a trail, Marley reflected how this was diametrically counter to his Special Ops training. When you were inserted in country, you stuck to the slopes so as not to be an obvious target. But times and situations were different, if only in degrees.

Guzmán looked back at the odd assortment of buildings in the valley. The mist now shrouded the area. Vague outlines of the structures could be discerned inside the cloudy covering. The gray vault sparkled as if lit from within.

❋ ❋ ❋

3:33am

After a long night of walking they crested another rise, and below them they could see the outlines of cookie-cutter houses. Beyond the houses to the left was the actual Lake Elsinore of the town of the same name. The sub-division looked serene in the pre-dawn light.

"Too late for this to be my life." Guzmán looked fondly on the scene below. "And I'm not even thirty."

"I have a feeling you'd find it boring."

"Getting shot at every three minutes gets on your nerves too, Marley."

He motioned for her to follow him. They clambered over a wooden fence and worked their way between identical tract houses, emerging onto a street devoid of trash or cracks in the sidewalks.

"Like out of that movie," Guzmán remarked, "*Pleasantville.*"

"And just like modern suburbia to have all the Goddamn cars put away at night." Marley looked up then down the street. There were no vehicles in sight.

"All these places have attached garages you can enter from the house."

"There's got to be something."

"There better be." He started walking toward a corner, hands thrust in his pockets.

"Or what?" She slipped an arm around his. "You going to break into someone's crib to get to their car?"

His look told her he'd weighed such an option. "That's not a situation I can control. There may be kids, a pet, who knows. Hell, the way our luck's been running, granny might come out of the back room and blow us away with the family six-shooter."

She was about to reply when they heard an engine. Quickly they hid behind a large clump of birds-of-paradise. An older Dodge pick-up truck rounded the corner. There were intermittent gray puffs of oil coming from the tailpipe. From the bed, a kid threw the morning newspaper. The street was a cul-de-sac, and the truck would have to do a U-turn to leave the way it had come.

They watched the truck roll past.

"Talk to the driver," Marley said, having noticed the man at the wheel was Latino. "I don't want to spook him or make him think we're going to hurt his kid. Tell him we'll give him this to rent the truck." He peeled off two twenties and gave them to her. There were other bills. This was money he'd found stuffed in the fake vampire's pockets. "Tell him he can pick it up at Prima Storage on Sycamore in Santa Ana after nine this morning."

"On it." Guzmán flagged the man down as he came back around. She showed him the money and pointed to where Marley had wisely decided to stand in the open. Guzmán and driver exchanged more words, then she signaled for Marley to come over.

"I got us a bargain, Marley," she said in Spanish. "Ruben here and his son, Frank, will drive us to our location for a hundred."

"And the catch?" Marley asked, also in Spanish. He could see it coming.

"We help him finish his route."

Marley made a sound, but decided making a fuss would only lose him a ride. The "we" part consisted of Guzmán riding in the cab with Ruben, laughing and chatting away. Marley and Frank had to do all the real work of throwing the papers. But they passed the time talking about baseball, and Marley learned a lot about the intricacies of Pokémon cards. You never knew when such information might be valuable.

Nonetheless, the job got done, and on their way to Santa Ana, they dropped Frank off at school. Marley paid the man the hundred, tipped fifty, and wished them *buena suerte* as he drove away from Prima Storage.

The familiar sound of rotor blades had them crane their necks as a helicopter went by high overhead.

8:13am

"Looks like recess is over."

8:34am
Santa Ana, Orange County

Marley checked the time on his battered Elgin watch as they left Prima Storage. "Hold on, okay?"

"What choice do I have?" Guzmán squeezed her arms tight around his lower torso.

Marley's foot clicked the clutch into first on the Kawasaki 1000 motorcycle, the model used by the LAPD. He preferred his racing Ducati, but you couldn't ride two on one of those bad boys. And this bike had been bored out to 1300 ccs for more speed, so it would do. He took off down the street. It felt good to be wearing fresh clothes. The sun glinted off his round Torque shades. Even their grub of microwaved breakfast burritos and donkey piss coffee had been welcome.

A motorcycle was a vulnerable conveyance. But he was going to encounter a lot of morning traffic and would need the bike's greater mobility to reach Los Angeles on time.

"We're going to make it, aren't we, Marley?" The Kawasaki was equipped with proper dampeners, so she didn't have to shout.

"No day is a good one to die," he said. "You just make sure that bag doesn't come loose, Lina."

New, fully functional guns and a few other pieces of ordnance were in an equipment bag, the strap draped bandolier-style across her upper body.

"You just make sure you don't crash this thing," she said.

He guided the motorcycle into the traffic flow of the 5 Freeway heading north. The Kawasaki fell in behind a semi, and he maneuvered to the lane next to the truck. When and where he could, Marley split traffic by zooming through the spaces between cars stacking up in rush hour. More than once, the remains of hot lattes were nearly dumped on them as people emptied their cups through open windows. And one woman nearly sideswiped them as she talked nonstop on her cell phone. As for attackers, there was a break. A condition neither of the two knew would last for long.

9:01am

They crossed the L.A. County line around 9:15. Shortly thereafter, they neared Norwalk.

"Traffic's looser on the freeway now," Marley said. "They could come at us again." Not waiting for a response, he took to the street.

"You think this will be safer?"

"The odds, Lina. It's always about the odds and how they change constantly. If we're jammed up, we have a better chance of getting away if I can use side streets and alleys for cover."

"I suppose your girlfriends are going to take another run at us."

"Somebody will."

He took Imperial Boulevard paralleling the 105 Freeway heading west. They crossed Old River School Road near the Los Amigos Golf Course. Several motorcycles had been on the highway, but Marley's eyeballing and intuition discounted them as threats. But now there was a roar of other big bikes, and his internal alarms went off. The nerves at the base of his neck knotted up.

"Hold on tight. And while you're at it, see if you can get one of the pistols out of the bag."

"It fucking figures," Guzmán said. She tightened her legs around the seat and got the bag around in front of herself. "Don't you want me to use real firepower and get the shotgun out?"

"The recoil would knock us off the bike, or at least you." Marley's mouth was a tight line as he ratcheted the accelerator on the Kawasaki's handle. The bike shot forward smoothly. From behind a station wagon he could see one of the bikes, a Harley, zooming closer in his rear-view mirror. He braked suddenly, allowing a garbage truck to pull alongside, then go past them. Marley swerved into the lane where the truck was, almost causing a Volvo to slam into them.

"Asshole!" The man driving the Volvo yelled at Marley.

Guzmán screamed over the cacophony of engines and squealing brakes. "I got one of the guns out."

"Keep it low, but we'll need it soon enough." The first bike that peeled away from the station wagon bore down on them fast from their right rear. They had been lucky and had gone through two green lights in a row, but now they were coming to a red. Not too far beyond the signal was an access road leading down to the Los Angeles River that crossed Imperial.

"Since you have a thing about religion, now would be a good time to pray." He slipped the Kawasaki through the intersection against the red light. Tires screeched and horns blared. A Camry almost clipped their rear tire, and one car rear-ended another.

Guzmán had one arm around him, her hand on his flat stomach. The other hand held the gun, a Colt Delta Elite 10 mm, tight against his ribs. Coming at a perpendicular angle through the intersection was a transport truck hauling concrete sections of sewer pipe. The truck driver was standing on his brakes, his tires smoking white clouds.

"Oh shit, Marley!"

The Kawasaki found an opening between the throng of people who had foolishly believed they were safe crossing the street. Those people scattered as the bike tore though the busy intersection, and Marley clipped the heels of a woman running to get out of the way.

9:22am

"Oh, Jesus, terrorists!" she cried.

The big rig jackknifed, and the flat bed trailer swept along the sidewalk. The trailer slammed against a light post, slowing its momentum, and the light post snapped in two. People waiting at a bus stop rushed to safety as sections of concrete pipe rolled and demolished the bus shelter and storefronts.

As this happened, a Suzuki bearing down on Marley and Guzmán plowed into the side of a car that, in turn, got rear-ended. The rider went flying over the hood of the car and landed in a heap on the other side in the roadway.

A tricked-out, lowered black Explorer, rap song blaring from its Alpine stereo, braked but rammed into the

Suzuki's driver. He became lodged in the SUV's under-carriage as the vehicle ground to a halt, his cries of pain drowned out by the general chaos.

Two motorcyclists, on a Harley and BMW, were left to press their assault. This duo got through the tangle of the intersection and closed in on Marley and Guzmán. A shot boomed, and a bullet clipped the Kawasaki's fender.

"Time to rock," Marley said, juicin' the bike.

"Oh, you've just been warming up so far," she cracked. Guzmán pumped off two rounds at the motorcycles coming after them but didn't hit anything.

Marley took the access road downhill. At the bottom was a chain-link fence and beyond that, the L.A. River. As he fishtailed the bike into a fence along a narrow path, more shots rang out from their pursuers. Marley grunted as one tore into his side. He struggled with the bike as it tipped. Guzmán was almost knocked loose, and the gun fell out of her hand. She reached to get it, but they were already in motion again.

"Hey!" she bellowed in protest.

"I see an opening." The bike bore along the path. Marley clicked down the gears, using the clutch to slow the Kawasaki. They came to a ragged opening that had been cut and pulled back in the chain links. His foot slipped on the clutch bar, and he accidentally killed the engine.

"Hold tight." They had to bend down to get through the opening. More shots rang out, and he gasped.

"Marley, oh shit, you've been hit."

"Fuck it." He got them through, and they rode the machine down the slant of the wall to the concrete L.A. River bed. The rainfall had been sparse, so this time of year offered no surprises. They coasted to flat terrain, a thin sheet of water running down the middle of the so-called river. The other riders were almost to the opening.

She said, "Come on, come on."

The bike's electric starter caught on the second crank. "Garvin was on his J," Marley said, his breath coming up short.

The two riders cleared the opening. Guzmán dug in the bag for another pistol, but the shotgun was the only remaining gun. Her Beretta had been tossed away by the goth hit man.

"There's only this," she said, shaking the sawed-off Mossberg.

The wound in Marley's side was burning, the slug in him getting trounced around as the motorcycle went along. Shots blazed from behind them. One pinged off the Kawasaki's gas tank.

"Fuck," Guzmán bellowed, almost tumbling off the rear.

"I'm going to try something," Marley said. "Hold on to me as tight as you can."

She managed to latch parts of her arms around his

9:25am

shoulders just as he sent the bike into a tight turn. The bike leaned precariously, and Marley had to use his left leg as a brace to keep them from tipping over. The back tire of the Kawasaki churned, and the frame shook as the bike completed its vicious arc, partly climbing up the embankment wall.

The Harley followed him. The expediter brought the Kawasaki around as this man aimed a Glock at them. He tossed the surprise he'd been saving. Instinctively, the driver dropped his pistol and caught the grenade, and he and his motorcycle were blown to hell in great, fiery chunks. Marley raced through the gray and black plumes saturating the air.

The last attacker was up in the seat of his bike, his left hand working the brake lever as he sighted with the gun in his right fist.

Marley righted the bike coming off the wall. Guzmán lost her grip and tumbled off. The shotgun slid along the concrete bed of the L.A. River. This only registered to him dully as he charged the other biker. A shot grazed the white streak in his hair as he lowered his body and tore full speed at the other man and his oncoming bike.

As he'd anticipated, the attacker had to stop firing and start maneuvering as Marley got closer. He swerved, and, as he did, Marley lashed out with his leg, catching the other man in his breadbasket. This one doubled over but didn't fall off his motorcycle. The BMW came back around, the rider preparing to fire again.

A blast of buckshot shredded one side of the attacker's Polo leather jacket, and he went over sideways off his bike. His motorcycle skidded, sending sparks everywhere. Marley got off his motorcycle, giving Guzmán the high sign for a job well done. He trotted to the wounded man, his own injury tamped down by his adrenalin.

The attacker was now on his stomach, reaching for his pistol. He drew a chrome-plated Smith & Wesson .380.

Marley put a foot on the gun. Guzmán came limping closer.

"Now what, fool?" Marley picked up the gat and aimed it at the man on the ground. Part of the man's side was reddened, his breathing ragged beneath his helmet. He looked up at the two, their forms reflected in his scraped visor.

"Off." Marley jerked the gun at him.

He complied and took off his helmet. He was blonde with three earrings in one lobe and a diamond encrusted nose stud.

"Where's Twelvetrees?" Marley asked in a pleasant tone.

"Suck my dick, bitch," the other man said.

Guzmán was about to put the barrel of the Mossberg on him, but Marley waved her off. "Gosh, let's not resort to such barbaric tactics, huh, Lina?" Marley's features were unreadable.

9:28am

"Maybe you couldn't hear me the first time, my friend." Marley leaned over slightly. The bullet agitated his side, but he showed a stoic face. "We'd like it if you'd be so kind as to inform us as to the whereabouts of Samson Twelvetrees. I'm sure you're supposed to report in to him."

"Maybe you got shit between your ears, faggot mother-fuckah," the other man spat at him. "I ain't telling you or your ho a Goddamn thing."

Marley chuckled. "If that's the way you feel about it." A remorseless expression descended on him, and he stepped closer to the man. Three Earrings set himself. Marley ground his foot in the man's upper body where he'd been nailed by the shotgun. Guzmán looked away as the man screamed in pain.

"Nobody's gonna save you. Nobody's even gonna hear you over the traffic going by." His own wound was starting to get to him, but he had to front, had to maintain his iceman demeanor.

"Where the hell is Twelvetrees?" He let the pressure up.

"A number, a number is all I got," Three Earrings blubbered. "I swear to God, man."

"You supposed to report in, is that it?"

"Yeah, got a cell on the bike."

"Then make it so."

Guzmán fetched the cell phone from a compartment beneath the BMW's seat. She and Marley, trying not to show his discomfort, marched the man into one of the recessed tributary tunnels in the embankment.

"Call in," Marley commanded the thug. He leaned against the tunnel wall. He was starting to show wear, his face losing color.

"Sure," the other man said. His eyes shifted from Marley to Guzmán and the Mossberg she was holding.

Marley put the pistol against Three Earring's temple. "I ain't fadin' out, so don't you."

The man considered his options and punched in the number. "Let me speak to Twelvetrees, this is Busey," he said when the call connected.

As they'd told him, he put the cell phone to Guzmán's ear. She listened as a new voice came on the line. "Yes, I hope you're calling with good news, Busey."

Guzmán nodded her head in the affirmative and let Busey talk. She shoved the shotgun barrel under his chin.

"He was good, took out Harrelson and Farley, but I bagged his ass." Busey listened, holding the phone so Marley could hear too. "Yeah, I know where it is," Busey said after Twelvetrees had stopped talking. "I'll meet y'all there." He clicked the phone off.

"We square?" Three Earrings was also starting to look peaked. The fear of being shot was now overtaken by the damages of his own wound. "I did what you want. You got a location for Twelvetrees."

"He might send a gopher, son." Marley seemed to draw energy from the other man's apprehension. He stood erect, his voice unwavering.

"Man, I can't do nothin' about that. I got to see a doc just like you do."

"But we drop your blonde butt at a hospital, you might 411 us to Twelvetrees." He held out his hand and Guzmán gave him the shotgun. He racked it. The sound reverberated off the tunnel walls, making the other man grimace.

9:35am

"Oh, shit, Marley." Horror strained the man's features in the half light of the tunnel. "You supposed to be cool, man. You the one I heard about got them UN hostages out of that situation in Kosovo, right?"

"How you hear that?"

"I was in the Rangers. You know, parachute in, parachute out, and all that shit."

"Yeah, all that shit." Marley knocked him senseless with the end of the shotgun.

"He might bleed to death." Guzmán remarked as she walked beside Marley back into the sunlight.

"He might," Marley answered. "But I damn sure will if you don't get me to L.A."

She looked at him in wonder. "You're asking me for help?"

"You help me, you help yourself."

"Fuck you, tough guy." She started to walk away.

Marley laughed. "You know how to drive a motorcycle?"

She whirled around. "You're not in any shape to do it, are you?"

"You need me to get to Sacramento alive."

Small drops of blood dotted the concrete around Marley's feet. They stared at one another, each not willing to give too much to the other — for fear they'd give too much.

Finally Guzmán said, "Come on, Marley, you still have to earn your big faces."

"Sure you right."

She supported him, and the two walked along the concrete river until they arrived at another access tunnel. The walls of the tunnel were covered in *placas* from gangs and tagger crews. On the other end they came out facing a large, fenced-in yard of orange-colored trucks and forklifts.

"Some kind of city facility."

"You don't look so good," Guzmán said, her brows crunched.

"I'll make it." He walked to a locked gate in the fence and got it open with the slim blade. The effort took a lot out of him, and he drooped against the fence.

"Can you get one of these trucks going?" Guzmán helped him as they snuck across the yard. She also carried the equipment bag, the pistols, and shotgun inside of it.

"Yeah," he said.

"Hey, can I help you?"

The two turned to a beer-gut man in an orange vest and hard hat. He was carrying a clipboard and looked very irritated.

"This is a restricted area," the city worker said. "You need to be on official business or be gone."

Marley reached into his back pocket. "We are. Let me show you."

The worker noticed the wetness on Marley's side, even through the dark color of the Shaka King three-quarter length jean jacket. Instinctively, he started backing up. "Hey, what's going on here?"

The yard man started to shout, and Marley clipped him with a swift blow of the point of his Prada shoe to the man's forehead. He staggered and Marley clocked him with a straight left. The couple hurried and found a pick-up truck between two dirt haulers.

9:43am

Marley got behind the wheel. Using a screwdriver lying on the seat, he thrust it into the ignition switch and got the truck started.

"You better let me drive," Guzmán said.

Marley was going to protest but reconsidered. They switched seats. There was a commotion. The man they'd jumped had been found, and now several workers were running around looking for the intruders.

"There they are," some dude shouted. "They're stealing Larry's truck."

"Get this bucket moving." Marley reached for the Smith & Wesson in the bag.

Guzmán ground the clutch, getting the transmission into reverse. She backed up, making two of the workers scatter. One of them grabbed her arm through the driver's window.

"Be cool." Marley aimed over his head and shot, and the city worker let go.

Guzmán bumped into a bulldozer, righted the truck, then made for the exit. The worker's enthusiasm about stopping the thieves had been chilled once they heard the gunshot. They shouted at the two as the truck drove away.

"You know how to get to L.A.?" Marley grimaced and adjusted his body in the seat.

"I got a crib in the Santa Monica Mountains, home. Laid, ya know what I'm saying." She smiled at him. "I use it for business meetings throughout the year. And don't trip, the leases are all under false names and dummy corporations that I took care of myself.

"We can light there. If Twelvetrees thinks you're dead, he'll probably call off his posse from watching the place."

"Sounds right." She shifted into high gear and got them onto the freeway. "Won't the cops be looking for us in this truck?"

"Yeah." Marley sounded tired. "But I'm bettin' a stolen city vehicle ain't a high priority until they link this with the pile up we caused."

"We? You're the one-man demolition squad."

Marley patted her cheek and let his head slump against the window. He sat very still as Lina Guzmán drove on, the sun in the sky rising bright and high, suggesting a day of promise.

9:46am

MALIBU

10:33am
Malibu, California

"Yo, dawg, you gettin' some of that?" Coleridge smelled of Glen Eden Scotch and two-day-old funk. He had a square robot-like head atop a once-robust frame going to sag. There was a spot of steak sauce on his paisley-patterned vest.

"Man, just get this Goddamn slug out of me, aw'rite?" Marley put his head back on the pillow atop the massive Ethan Allen oak bed. He lay with his shirt off on floral print sheets, an expensive comforter on the floor.

One large wall of the bedroom was a curved window allowing a panoramic view of the Pacific Ocean. Between the sea and the window were other multi-million dollar homes planted along the hill. This was one of Lina Guzmán's well-appointed houses she maintained in the Americas, Europe, and the Caribbean.

Malibu was a trendy enclave of mostly "industry"—

that is, Hollywood—types. The latest Mercedes or Lexus SUVs occupied driveways where oils stains were scrubbed meticulously clean by their minimum wage Latino help.

How incongruous that Marley's world should invade a place the natives fought hard to keep as a refuge from the likes of him. It was okay that someone like Lina Guzmán should be a denizen. Yeah, the dish was she made her money in a gangsterish fashion, but she was cultured, well-spoken, and only around infrequently. Nothing like the street riff-raff who actually sold her product. Though quiet as it's kept, many of the residents of Malibu smoked more than their fair share of the rock. They just didn't bear the brunt of such behavior as those of the ghettos and barrios did.

10:40am

Coleridge looked through his probes and forceps and scalpels, whistling as his long, thick fingers picked up this instrument or that. "Would you go into the bathroom and soak a couple of towels in warm water, young lady?"

"Sure." Guzmán left the room.

Coleridge said quietly to Marley, "I should hear soon from our old contacts about that matter you asked me to inquire about."

"Yeah." Marley lay with his arm on his forehead.

Coleridge settled on a scalpel with a rounded head. The medical tools were laid out on paper towels from the kitchen, the acute smell of rubbing alcohol emanating from the sterilized instruments. "How's her mama look? If the old girl's got anything left, I got to push up on that. Dahmmn."

"Shut up, you nasty old crocus sack." Marley had to keep from laughing. Coleridge had to be sixty if he was a day, and at least four times divorced that Marley knew of.

When Guzmán came back into the room, Coleridge's ravenous eyes watched her over his rimless glasses.

"Take another jolt," Coleridge said.

Marley sat up and grabbed the glass of Cutty from the night stand. He swallowed a goodly amount and put the tumbler back. "Sorry about your sheets," he said to Guzmán.

"Don't worry about those." She smiled at Marley, then asked Coleridge, "Where should I put these?"

"Good, those are nice and big, good," he harped. He moved back from Marley. "Put that green one around the wound, leaving me room to dig the bullet out of our boy."

She leaned over to do it, and Coleridge bit his lips gazing at her firm backside.

"Check yourself," Marley warned him.

Guzmán pinched Marley's face and whispered to him. "Save your strength." She kissed him and then withdrew.

Coleridge had already taken off his shapeless suit jacket and rolled up his sleeves. Old marks from hypodermic needles were evident at the crooks of both his elbows. He now had a set of long-nosed tweezers in his other hand. "Hold him down," he told Guzmán.

She got a knee onto the bed and pressed her hands on Marley's shoulders. Coleridge went to work, whistling again.

Marley reared up as the tweezers dug into his wound. He ground his teeth to keep from crying out as the burly man searched in his side for the bullet.

"Hold still, brother man, I believe I've got something."

"Just make sure it ain't my intestines you're yanking on." Marley gasped as the tweezers went even deeper. His biceps bunched, and his fingers gripped the mattress, digging in.

"You let me handle my business, pardner." Coleridge grunted, employing the scalpel in one hand, the tweezers in the other.

"Hang on," Guzmán murmured. She kissed his forehead and wiped it with a washcloth.

Marley's leg twitched, and it felt as if a branding iron

were being gorged in his guts. He ground his teeth and held back a yell working its way up to his throat.

"Got it," Coleridge announced. He held the bloody misshaped slug aloft for all to see. "You still a lucky motherfuckah, Marley, the bullet's intact. Now clean him up with that other towel, darling."

Guzmán cleaned the area and took the towels away. Coleridge said, "Ha," and extracted a bottle and tufts of cotton from his red-white-and-blue bowling bag. It was the same bag in which he'd transported his other doctoring items.

"This local anesthetic should help the pain." He put some of the contents of the bottle on the cotton and dabbed it on the throbbing wound.

10:51am

"Why the fuck didn't you use that shit before?" Marley snapped.

"I forgot I had it, homey," Coleridge chuckled. He got an air-powered medical staple gun out of the bag. "By the time I remembered, I was already digging around."

"Goddammit, Coleridge, can't you keep your mind off pussy for more than five minutes?"

"Hey," the man shrugged, "if you wanted a real doctor who still had his license, you wouldn't have called me, now would you?" He began to staple the wound closed. "But my one bit of Hippocratic advice would be not to move around much for the next eight hours or so."

Guzmán came back in the room, watching Marley. She leaned on the doorway, absently playing with the end of her hair.

Marley was sitting up. He checked his ancient Elgin as Coleridge bandaged his handiwork. "It's already four to eleven." He made a disapproving sound.

"Then we don't make it," Guzmán said, walking more into the room.

"Yes, we will," Marley vowed. "We change the rules of engagement."

Coleridge smiled a knowing grin and wrapped gauze

around the other man's muscular abdomen. "Like old times," he said, a distant quality in his voice. "We made it through some rough ones, you rusty fossil."

"Like it or not, you gonna have to be careful, young blood. Even you bleed."

Guzmán put an arm around the expediter's shoulders. "What do I owe you?" she said to Coleridge.

"Me and him will tighten that up." He started to put his tools away. "Change that dressing in four hours if you can." He plunged a hand in his vest pocket and extracted a half-smoked Hoyo de Monterey Robusto cigar. He lit it with a battered gold Zippo. There was some sort of design in relief on the lighter, and Coleridge gazed at the seal before he put the lighter away again.

"*Buena suerte*," he said to both of them and walked out.

"How do you know these characters, Marley?" She pushed him back on the bed.

"Like I said, Ms. Guzmán, I'm a pro."

"Okay, don't answer. But you're getting your strength back, right?" She stood on the side of the bed, pulling her sleeveless Poleci light sweater over her head.

"This will slow us down, Ms. Guzmán."

"I like it slow and, on occasion, fast, Marley." She unhooked her bra and slid beside the recuperating man.

"What about our appointment?" He groaned, but nonetheless unbuckled his pants, his hard-on prominent as she unzipped him.

"Fuck Twelvetrees, Saunders, and they mamas. Like you said, let's change the game." She took him in her mouth, and pinwheels went off behind Marley's eyes.

10:59am

11:49am
Back at It

A little later, Marley was lapping on one of her nipples. A breeze blew in from the sliding glass door that Guzmán had cracked open. The air caressed their cooling naked bodies. A Mary J. Blige ballad played softly on the Teac.

"Marley," she murmured, her fingers gently massaging the top of his close-cut hair.

"Umm," he mumbled, his mouth and tongue busy on her areola.

"Is that your first or last name?"

Playfully he bit her nipple. "I can't remember."

She was about to say something when the cell phone they'd taken from Busey rang. Marley stopped what he was doing and rolled over on the bed for the device.

"Careful, you'll bust your stitches," she said, keeping an arm around his taut waist.

"Staples," he corrected and clicked on the phone. "Besides," he growled in a low tone, "they held while you were riding me."

He answered the phone. "Marley. What's crackin'?"

"I got the shiznit on the hizzy where they's layin' in the cut, yo. I scoped 'em from that loc you gave me, feel what I'm saying?"

"Good work, Mad-T. Four large plus a deuce bonus for putting me in the pocket."

"Right, right."

Mad-T dropped the address and Marley clicked off. He got up and started getting dressed. The staples had to hold, at least 'til he got to Samson Twelvetrees. "That other call I made when we were coming here paid off. My man Mad-T followed one of Twelvetrees's knuckleheads from the place where he was supposed to meet Busey."

11:51am

"Then won't he know something's up by Busey not being there?"

"Yeah, but he won't know exactly what yet. He's gotta send some troops out to find Busey. So now's a time to go at 'em."

Guzmán slipped on black satin VS panties. "So much for romance." She got serious. "We can walk away right now, Marley." She stood there, glistening in the morning light, a combination of sex goddess and international crime lord. "Me and, well, at least twenty to thirty million I can scrape together."

Marley had his pants on. "That won't eliminate the threat."

"Those ducats buy us a lot of bodyguards and fancy fortification, Marley. We can have an island all to ourselves."

In her closet she had several men's shirts hanging up. Idly, he imagined who the garments had been for as he reached for one. "Always looking back ain't my thing, Lina."

"Go at the problem, eliminate the problem. You sound like my father."

"He must have had his good points then." He buttoned up a loose cotton shirt, but left the tail hanging.

"Well maybe I say *nada más*, Marley. Maybe I pull the plug on this crazy shit right now. I tell Saunders to shove his deal up his tight white ass, and I'm through with everything. You included if need be."

Marley paused as he got his kicks on. He wasn't going to show it, but the sexual workout—and it had been a

world-class gymnastics tournament—had taken a lot out of him. But there was no stopping now.

"You make your own decisions, Ms. Guzmán. I've made mine." He stood and could feel one of the staples loosening. "But we got a chance to take it to him, and to stop having clowns tryin' to punk us."

Coleridge had, upon Marley's request, delivered another Sig Sauer P226 and extra ammo. He clipped on a belt holster the unlicensed MD had also brought. He hid that and the gun under the long tail of the shirt. He put the shells in his pockets. "I can use one of your rides, right?" He held out his hand, expectant.

"You're so—" she gestured manically.

A self-satisfied smile settled on his mug.

She got out a set of keys from the night stand but held onto them. "Fuck it, I guess I'm in."

"You sure?"

"Shit yeah." She got the rest of her clothes on. They left the house in her late-model, turquoise Jaguar S-Type.

"Might as well get in the mood." He turned on her Jensen CD, the speakers bumping a mellow tone. Here he was, a rich hottie next to him, at the wheel of her flossy whip, and he'd in effect just turned down twenty million to go away with her and make love 'til they got bored— and the Goddamn Raiders would win another Super Bowl before he got tired of doing that. What was wrong with him?

"You're strange, you know that?" she said. "You're going to meet the enemy, and you play music."

11:59am

"Relaxing helps my mind focus." Marley made a call on the cell phone as he drove. He talked as the smooth running machine headed east through the tunnel leading into Santa Monica.

She opened the glove compartment and undid a hidden latch. A lid opened under the dash, revealing a plastic bag of powdered coke. She took out the bag and deftly put some of the 'caine on the edge of her finger.

He eyed her peripherally as Guzmán genteelly snorted some of her own product. "Not too much, you have a role to play, ya know?"

"I understand." She sniffed and put her bag away. "I didn't want to insult you and offer you a taste. I figure you more of a single malt and Arturo Fuente man."

"Close enough," he said, going around a Taurus with a badly faded paint job on the 10 Freeway.

"Unless," she licked in his ear, "you'd like me to put some blow on the head of your dick and suck it." She rubbed her hand on his upper thigh.

"We got to keep on our business, Ms. Guzmán." But he didn't remove her hand.

The digital clock on the dash read: 12:02. The cell chimed, and Marley snapped it up. He listened, then rang off. "Twelvetrees is holed up in some kind of office in an industrial park in South Gate. You know anything about that?"

"Fuck." Guzmán hit the dashboard.

Marley made a face. "I guess that's a yes."

"It's one of my transfer stations."

"That might be *was*," Marley corrected.

She glared menacingly at him. "You know about South Gate, Mister I-know-every-Goddamn-thing? You know what's been happening in Southeast L.A., in places like Huntington Park, Bell Gardens, Maywood, Cudahy, and all that?"

"I got the feeling you're about to take me to school, girl."

"I am," she shot back. "Southeast L.A. is a booming economy and a booming population."

"Lot of crackers out there back in the day," he noted. "Them oakies coming out 'cause of the dust bowl and all that way back in the '30s."

"Thank you for the ancient history."

"My pleasure."

"I should slap you. Anyway, as I was saying, this growth has happened, yet it's invisible to the white world. The good ol' boys who used to sit on those local elected seats down there have been replaced by Latino politicians and activists. Business and industry has blown up among the *eses*."

"What you're really telling me is all these new faces mean you have your crews in place too. And that it makes sense to have your product move through there. And I would guess a lot of money laundering is going on down there too."

"Exactly. So we're going into territory I know but that's now up for grabs. And that means we can't go in there blasting away."

"I didn't intend for us to do that." He winced as a pain lanced through his side when the car hit a bump. "Twelvetrees is plotting his next moves too. I'm hoping they ain't found Busey yet, or maybe the cops have already nabbed him."

"But he knows I'm not dead yet."

"That's why you're gonna call him." He handed her the cell phone.

12:04pm

She didn't even blink. "What do you want me to say?"

"You want to cut a deal. Call the dogs off and all that shit."

"He'll know it's a trap."

"Yeah, he's no mark. On the other hand, he ain't gonna let the opportunity pass him by, I reckon."

"He's got the upper hand, Marley."

"But he's still got to be worked about you being in a position to talk to Saunders or some other law dog and maybe disrupt part of the operation he's bogarted from you. He's a businessman, and like all bidness men, he wants to have as little static about his shit as possible." Marley powered the car into the fast lane. "The reality is, alive, you're still too much of a liability."

"So you want me to invite him to kill me?"

Marley beamed at her like a schoolboy. "Uh-huh."

They went over her lines, and she dialed the number Marley had memorized when Busey called Twelvetrees. The line picked up after the third ring.

"Let me speak to Samson." Guzmán put bass in her voice. She listened, then, "Tell him it's Lina, mother-fuckah."

"Don't overdo it," Marley said.

She stuck her tongue out at him. Twelvetrees came on.

"So pleased to hear from you too, Samson ... yeah,

that's right, we peeled a cap on all them sorry scrubs you sent against me and my man."

She started laughing silently. Marley grimaced at her, but she pretended to ignore him.

"You know perfectly well why I'm callin'," she said, interrupting Twelvetrees. "I got a proposition, so shut the fuck up and listen. You put a leash on your hounds, and I won't snitch to Saunders, period."

She listened, her foot tapping the floorboard. "Yeah, yeah, hell no. It's not your worry about where my *lana's* coming from. You may have hijacked my operation, but a girl's got to have some secrets."

Twelvetrees replied, and she gave him the final enticement as she and Marley had discussed.

"Meet me in forty minutes in the 'hood at Avalon and 50th, in the gym there at South Park. And I'll give you the name of the freighter out on the ocean now with 100 mil in product."

She listened. "Of course you don't know about it, Samson. I didn't get here yesterday."

Marley could tell Twelvetrees was squawking, and he signaled for Guzmán to hang up.

"39 minutes, and I better see your sorry ass there, or this offer is off the table." She broke contact and tossed the phone in the back seat. "Well?"

"Best we can do, homegirl. Now we see if his greed eats at him, and our luck's still good."

"I know it is. That was smart having me make up that

story about the ship." She massaged the back of his neck with her fingertips.

See? he chastised himself. Do the nasty with a client, and already she's going on like they were Will and Jada. Like they actually had a shot at a future together when they both knew that wasn't very likely.

He made a stop on a residential street at a nondescript clapboard house in Santa Monica. In five minutes, he returned to the car with two loaded Trader Joe's grocery bags, a woman in curlers and a bathrobe waving at him from the doorway. Guzmán just shook her head.

12:08pm

Back up on the 10 freeway, they came to the interchange where the 110, the Harbor Freeway, branched off to the 10. Marley switched lanes, taking the 110 south.

The Harbor Freeway was a conduit that cut through the ghetto of L.A. proper, then continued further south to Watts and the city of Compton. These areas had once been predominantly black but now had given way to a Latino population that was a majority in numbers but not in voting power. Yet that too was changing. And

unless people figured out how to get along and realize the crumbs they were snatching from one another wasn't the whole pie they hadn't baked, then it would always be a ghetto.

"Where're you from, Marley?"

Her question broke him out of his musings. "Nowhere, baby."

"You just showed up one day a full-grown man."

"Feels like it sometimes," he said. The Jaguar flowed into light traffic leading to their destination. Neither of them said another word until they arrived at South Park.

A few brothers and *vatos*, unemployed or merely skipping school, were playing B'ball. And some old men, with elongated faces like Yoruba masks, were slapping domino tiles and sipping beer in front of the rec center. The hoorahing of the men drifted to them as Marley slowly went past, window down, checking out the area.

"Christine Maples," one old-timer exclaimed, placing a bone that got him fifteen points.

"That ain't shit, gimme twenny, sco' keeper."

Marley drove toward the San Pedro end of the park, behind the gym attached to the rec center. He turned into a driveway and parked. The two got out. There was no access door on the rear, and Marley led the way to a side of the building where the fire door was located. He got it open with a tool from his lock kit, but there was a chain around the bar on the other side.

"The front then." Guzmán pointed the way.

"We got to get them old-timers out of the way." Marley walked to the front and interrupted the players. "Fifty each, gents, and y'all stay away for an hour."

One of the men, wearing a Kangol cap, watched the game while perched on a plastic milk crate. He fish-eyed the newcomer. "You the one rolled by in that fancy car with that Mex gal next to you. What you up to, son?"

"A hundred, then." Time was a commodity he couldn't bargain about.

"Let's see it," another one said.

Marley produced the money and distributed the goods to each of the old-timers.

"Niggah, how I know this shit is real?" The one on the crate held one of the fifties to the sun as if he could recognize a fake bill.

"You don't. But I'll bet you'll take that chance for a paid

hour tax-free against what you must be getting from social security."

"Shit, I gets a pension from the Santa Fe Railroad, ya slick hustler." Guzmán walked up and the old boy's dentures all but fell out of his head.

Fortunately, a more reasoning individual spoke. "Come on, Robes, you know you can get your grandson a new video game with the money." He was a reedy man in thick horn-rimmed glasses, the one who had gotten the fifteen points in the game.

12:33pm

"I suppose," Robes started, eager to argue over some other minuscule point. But the other men were up and moving off, so he complied and went too. "Don't be tearing up this rec center," he said walking away. "The young folks in this neighborhood ain't got a lot, hear?"

"I know," Marley concurred. He picked the lock on the front, and the two went inside.

Ten minutes later, two identical, cobalt blue Lincoln Continentals cruised into South Park like land sharks sniffing out fresh chum.

12:44pm
The 'Hood

"I sure as hell don't like this." Maurice adjusted his mohair coat. And, as if it were a ritual, touched his glasses.

"You've made yourself completely clear, repeatedly." Samson Twelvetrees unlimbered his tall solid body from the car. He was dressed suburban casual in Bill Blass slacks, a loose shirt, and a suede sport coat. If not for the short stock Uzi strapped strategically under his coat, he could be a banker on a junket to check out investment possibilities in the "other" L.A.

Twelvetrees said to his lieutenant, "But I can end this now, my way."

Six additional men of various races and sizes, including Dee-Ray, piled out of the two vehicles. They all wore shades.

"Take those off, so you can see," Twelvetrees told his

crew. "You're not auditioning for a part in the next LL Cool J movie."

In unison, the men lost the shades and awaited further instructions.

The gents shooting hoops on the court had stopped playing and watched the tableau unfold. Shootouts of the bullet kind were not unknown in South Park.

"Front and rear, gentlemen," Maurice commanded. He produced a Gold Cup .45 ACP as the three marched toward the rear. "Dee-Ray, the door."

12:45pm

Dee-Ray moved lightly for a man his size. He snatched open the rec center door, finding only a gloomy interior.

"Twig," Maurice said, pointing.

One of the other muscle men in a Puma hoody stepped up and shined a halogen flashlight into the rec center. "Don't see shit yet." Twig stepped inside.

There was silence, then he stumbled back out, dropping the light. He pin-wheeled around, a surprised look on his unshaven face. He clawed at his chest then plopped onto the ground.

Twelvetrees had the Uzi in his hand, crouching behind the Lincoln. "What?"

Dee-Ray slammed the door shut and crouched down to his dead homey. "Some kind of dart sticking over Twig's heart. Damn, must be poisonous like in a Tarzan movie."

"Cheeky bugger, always full of surprises." Maurice adjusted his glasses, crouching near his boss. "We brought some C-4—let's blow him to kingdom come."

Twelvetrees stood again. "'Cause Marley won't have her in there, I know that."

"So, we get rid of him at least."

"We'll do this," Twelvetrees decided. "We coordinate our attack. We go through front and back at the same time and catch him in the cross fire. But we need to keep him alive long enough to tell us where Lina is hidden. Tell the men."

"Okay." Maurice got a few explosive packs out of the

trunk of one of the Lincolns. Then he ran around back, only to discover that the other entrance was a side door. He got the men in position and soon returned to the front. The pale man used his cell like a walkie-talkie to communicate with Dee-Ray and the others. Maurice adhered one of the C-4 paks to the door and confirmed that the man on the side of the building had done the same. They synchronized the timers and got set.

The ball players were enthralled by this development. The old domino men peeked out from behind a mainte-nance shed.

"They's gonna fuck up the rec center," Robes of the Kangol said.

"You about to make like John Shaft with your arthritis and bad knees and stop them?" the one in thick glasses retorted.

Robes remained mum.

The dominos players watched as the charges went off, simultaneously blowing both doors to shards. The crews rushed inside the building, Twelvetrees leading the way through the smoke.

Running inside, he toppled a metal device mounted on a tripod. Nervous, Twelvetrees shot off a round, and some of his boys began firing randomly.

"Wait, wait," Twelvetrees yelled over the gunfire. The shooting stopped, and he swung a light on whatever it was that he'd bumped into. The thing was a square box with a hole in its center. It was what had shot Twig with the dart.

Crossing their wrists to point their guns and the flash-lights, the crew swept light all over the interior. Dust and smoke billowed everywhere. "Check the other rooms. There must be an office, bathrooms, showers, all that." Maurice squinted as he peered around.

Momentarily, Twelvetrees was convinced that their quarry was not in the building.

"Tricky, tricky," Maurice said.

A look of cold realization rippled across Twelvetrees's face.

"Get out, get the fuck out now!" he bellowed.

The boss man was already in motion when another explosion went off. This one brought down the rafters, and a man's head was crushed as a beam fell on him. There was another explosion that popped out the remaining glass in the rec center. Like rolling thunder, a rumble arose from the basement as the furnace caught fire. One section of the building went up in a mushroom of flame and sound.

12:47pm

"Marley!" Twelvetrees hollered. His voice was drowned out by the collapse of wood and steel and plaster. Parts of the roof of the rec center fell in. Four of the crew lay on the polished gym floor, killed either by the concussion of the blast or by flying debris. They looked like they had worked out too hard and passed out from exhaustion. Maurice was alive, but his leg had been broken in two places when a pipe whipsawed against his knee.

Outside, Marley emerged from behind one of the Lincolns. When the hitters had arrived, he'd been hiding behind the tool shed with the oldsters. Then, when Twelvetrees and his boys had rushed the rec center, he broke into the trunk of one of the Lincolns, figuring they'd be packing serious ordinance. And he used their own explosives against them.

"Now look what you done," Robes criticized. He and the other men were now walking over to the wreckage.

"Sorry," Marley said. "But I got bigger priorities." He could hear men moaning from inside and wanted to make sure he finished off Twelvetrees. But sirens could be heard approaching, plus there was that Goddamn schedule to keep.

"I'll pay for it." Lina Guzmán emerged from the pack of basketball players who were also coming over. The young men had agreed to hide her fine self behind them. She took off the sweatshirt and cap she'd been given to wear.

"She will," Marley assured the men, young and old, who looked dubiously at her. "But right now, we gotta jet." Marley and Guzmán jogged for her Jaguar. Some of his staples had come lose, but there was nothing he could do about it now. He got the car in gear, and rather than take a chance on getting pulled over as they left the scene, drove east on 48th Street toward Wall.

Marley found an empty driveway to a modest house and pulled in. Fancy cars were not unknown in this part of the 'hood, and he hoped they weren't too conspicuous.

Guzmán tugged on Marley's wrist to look at his watch. "12:48," she announced. The band of the watch had come loose, and she fussed with it to get the strap around his wrist. Marley watched her with a bemused expression.

"Hey, isn't this the same seal that was on Coleridge's lighter?" Engraved on the back of the watch was a design consisting of a skull with horns and an eye patch with laurel leaves on each side. Superimposed on the leaves was a pair of dice showing snake eyes. Latin words in Gothic script were arched over the image.

Marley gently took his watch and strapped it back on. "Maybe I'll tell you that story some other time."

"But time is all we have, darling." She kissed him. "With Twelvetrees dead, I'm free. Let's just keep going."

The sirens had died down. No doubt the entire area around the park was now cordoned off. The usual code of silence residents of the community had with the cops would be in effect. That would give them enough of a head start to make it away clean.

Marley started the car again but held off putting the tranny into reverse. "Let's be real, Lina. I ain't ready to settle down to the picket fence routine or whatever people do laying around a beach. And you know you ain't either."

"We could still have fun, years of it," She looked like a million bucks.

"I know. But we both know why you were willing to roll over on Twelvetrees. Sure it had something to do with him making his move like he did, but your deal was also a way to get rid of him, the competition."

"You judging me? I've done a lot of do good with my money." She thumped her breastbone with her fingers. "It's not just the money to me, Marley."

12:49pm

"Cut the shit, baby. We both live in this world. I know you'll keep building playgrounds and *clínicas*—that's your way of giving back. It's also a way of alleviating your guilt."

She slapped him. "Like you're so Goddamn holy."

He put the car in gear and backed into the street. "We'll get this done, and then you can do what you want. If you're gonna go straight, invest your dough in legit businesses, that's cool. If not," he shrugged his shoulders, "then like you said, I'm sure not one to talk."

"There's no time left."

"Sure there is." The mischievous twist of his lips worried her.

"Wha ...?" she started to say.

Before she could finish, Marley knocked her out with a left to the jaw that would have made Roy Jones Jr. envious.

1:56pm
2,003 Feet Over Lodi

Guzmán came awake groggily to the sound of an engine whining and the feel of hot wind across her face. She had a pounding headache, and her jaw was sore. It was at that moment she realized her body was tilting, and she was restrained. She had the impression she was in a big aquarium, but she was dry as toast. Then she clicked fully awake. "Dammit," she hollered. "Goddammit! Marley."

"Now's not the time to be offendin' de Lord." Marley struggled with the controls of the helicopter. Fumes filled the cabin, and he waved an arm to clear his vision.

"You idiot, I told you no air travel." She tried to strike him, but the chopper listed violently, and she was thrown away from him. "What's going on?" she managed to ask.

"The fuckin' Furys, I'm speculating. They tracked us from Compton Airport somehow. Them vicious chicken-heads fragged the 'copter with a Stinger missile." Some of the smoke had parted. Irrigated farmland was visible through the plastic bubble of the cockpit.

"I guess saying 'I told you so,' would be overkill right about now, huh?" Guzmán braced herself for a crash.

1:58pm

Marley made a guttural sound as he fought to control the injured craft. Fire had erupted inside the instrument panel. The helicopter continued its downward spiral.

"Get set, Lina, I'm going to try to bring her down in one piece."

"That's what I like about you, Marley, always a positive fuckin' attitude."

On the ground, the Furys could be seen running from some cover bordering the cultivated fields. Workers were booking for safer ground. Another Stinger flew toward the 'copter.

But the stick responded, and Marley yanked the aircraft out of its dive. The missile roared past the rear rudder.

"They're desperate, not even waiting for the up close and personal kill."

"That's comforting to know," Guzmán said.

The helicopter came in at a low angle over the treetops. Sparks sputtered from the control panel, and the blades suddenly quit. The chopper glided for an instant, then dropped like an elevator car whose cable had broken.

"Marley!" she screamed and covered her face.

Briefly, Marley glared into the leering face of death, looking for his reflection. Snapping out of it, he used whatever momentum he could squeeze from the hurtling machine and pulled back on the stick. The 'copter crashed through limbs and foliage, and came to a sudden, teeth-jarring stop inside a mass of topiary. The two were upside down in the cockpit, and they could hear boughs creaking under the weight of the destroyed aircraft.

Guzmán was terrified. "Get me out of this, Marley. Get me out of this thing." She was shaking, on the verge of panic.

"We're alive, Lina, be happy." He worked to get his seatbelt loose. He did and got himself into an upright position.

"I knew I'd have to pay," she blurted, holding herself.

Marley got her loose, and she started to punch him.

"Cut it out or I'll leave you for them bloodthirsty bitches." He kicked open one of the doors to the cockpit. "It's not far to drop."

Like a spoiled child, Guzmán didn't respond. She went limp rather than try to save herself.

"You better get your ass in gear, girl, or so help me you get left." He pulled on her, and reluctantly, she came to life.

Marley got himself positioned in the door, a patch of ground beneath them. "Okay," he said. "Try to not go tense."

He took a hold of her, and as one they plunged to the earth. Marley got to his feet and helped her up.

"Move."

They ran as another missile whistled through the air. The helicopter exploded in a flash. Tops of trees lit up in bonfires as flaming pieces dropped like rotting fruit.

"Ughh." Guzmán sagged against Marley as they ran.

"You've probably got a mild concussion," he said. They stopped, and he let her sit next to a tree.

She held her head. "Duh. Imagine that after getting punched, then falling from the sky."

Marley was already moving off. "Try to be quiet. I know that's hard for you."

"Fuck you, Marley."

He ran through the farm worker's makeshift camp of tents and lean-tos. Old women and young children ran around, screaming in fear. Pots and pans were knocked off open fires, and a barrel bar-b-que tipped over with its roasted pig on the spit. He reached the end of the thickets that let onto the agricultural fields of the northern end of the Central Valley. They were less than fifty miles from Sacramento, but it might as well be a thousand if he didn't step up. It was time to let these twists get served.

He took several steps, but the instinct that had kept him alive this long kicked in, and Marley hit the dirt. Rounds from twin handguns heated the air over him. He belly crawled forward to a tin shack that provided minimal cover. He could tell where the shooting was coming from, and he'd bet a wad of benjamins who the hot head firing was.

"'Zup, niggah?" LaNetta showed herself, stomping through the camp. She wore tight leather pants and platform tennis shoes. As usual, she was expertly spraying rounds of her twin Glocks at where she thought he was.

2:02pm

She kicked in parts of the tin shack and then looked for Marley's body behind it, but he'd bounced. "You got nowhere to hide up in this muh fuh, player."

"Pull back," Monique ordered her.

"Girlfriend, I know what the fuck I'm doing," she said into her headset. "Come on, Marley, let's get this over with. You always knew I was better than you. That's why you broke it off with me and took up with Nera." She traipsed along a narrow passage between some older bunk houses and a grove of trees.

"No, that's not it. I always knew your ego would trip you up one day, LaNetta." Marley stepped into the path she was on. "And if I stayed with you, me too." She brought her weapon up, grinning like a drunk. But he was faster. He pumped one right into her temple, just like he'd cooled her partner. The head shot was the only shot to take with the Furys. All their attire was woven with bulletproof material.

He ran forward, and flames suddenly consumed one of the bunk houses. At first he thought it had been another missile exploding. But there had been no sound, just the fire. *Flamethrower, shit.* Blocked from behind, he had no choice but to break into the open ground of the fields.

Marley ran diagonally across a rice paddy, splashing water with his thick-soled Red Wing boots.

Nikki, Nera's sister, in hip-hugging Speedos and a flattering spaghetti strap top, came into view.

"Hi, Marley." She aimed a stream of liquid fire at him from a black lacquer flamethrower strapped on her back. He avoided getting roasted by throwing himself behind a tractor.

Nikki was the fourth Fury and usually was the coordinator and driver of their high-tech van. She used her electronic gear to track their quarries. But his icing her big sister no doubt motivated her to get into the fight.

Nikki hosed down the tractor in streams of red and yellow. The gas tank went up, and she watched the gray smoke climb into the pretty blue sky.

2:05pm

"Almost sorry to see him go," she muttered.

Three shots boomed through the rising smoke. Two of the slugs ripped into her protected clothing. The third ignited her tank, and she went over backward, still staring at the sky as a fireball swallowed her whole.

Marley got out of the ditch he'd thrown himself in beside the tractor. He cleaned the dirt off his Sig as he trotted off, passing the crackling pit of fire that used to be Nikki.

Marley moved around the periphery of the trees lining the field. Monique had to have been the one using the Stinger launcher. But that wasn't a practical weapon for on-the-ground combat. Plus, he knew her, knew how she

liked to do her killing. If she found Guzmán, dazed like she was, she'd be dead by now. Monique didn't play; none of that hostage shit for her.

He crept back toward where he'd left Guzmán. Marley passed under a cluster of maples. A rifle crack sounded from above, and a bullet puffed a hole in the back of his jacket. Marley stumbled but managed to flop himself between some of the trees, flip over on his back, and fire.

Monique, dressed in camouflage pants and black tank top, dropped from above. Her .300 Magnum Arms rifle fell to the ground beside her. She ignored the jagged hole that Marley's Sig Sauer had poked in her deltoid.

Marley, up on his feet, tugged on the material under his ruined Baroni zippered wool jacket.

"I took my cue from you, Monique. Kevlar shirt, special order from my tailor on Crenshaw in L.A."

"So what?" She got her guard up.

He took off the jacket for greater mobility. He and Monique circled each other in their martial arts stances.

She tried a thrust with the edge of her knuckles. He blocked and struck with a blow that she thwarted. Marley answered with a lightning kick to her thigh. This backed her up.

"Like we were taught, huh?" She did a sweep trying to bring him down, but he tippy-toed out of her reach.

She rushed, and his boxing combination caught her. He tagged her with a left to her rib cage. She kicked his side, opening his wound more. Marley gritted his teeth but damn sure knew he couldn't show weakness.

Monique pressed the attack and got him twice behind the ear with the tip of her shoe. Marley felt woozy, sinking to his knees. The woman aimed a heel at his head. He rolled out of the way. Back on his feet, they exchanged a flurry of strikes, each one landing as many hits as the other.

The combatants parted, breathing hard through their bloody mouths. Monique tried an overhand lunge which Marley trapped. He threw a spin kick with his right leg, expecting her to duck. She did. He readjusted and gave her a chin-check with his left foot. Monique reeled. He caught her dead in the rib cage with the heel of his palm, cracking two. She lunged forward, but a knuckle strike on the bridge of her nose got her blinking. Marley followed with an elbow to the base of her skull, a blow designed to interrupt the brain signal for a millisecond.

She went down, dazed but still deadly. Marley raised his foot to snap her neck but hesitated. Guzmán came up.

"I think we've all had enough killing," she said.

Marley lowered his foot, nodding his head slightly. Guzmán stared at the body. Tattooed on Monique's bicep was the same symbol she'd seen on the back of Marley's watch and Coleridge's lighter. She wasn't going to ask him about it, because she wasn't going to get an answer.

2:11pm

He checked his Elgin. "We got time left."

"How do we get there?"

"In the Fury's battle van. It's got to be close by."

As they went in search of the vehicle, she said, "You know, don't you? From what I said about having to pay when we were in the helicopter. Why I was so afraid, so superstitious to be in one."

"Forget it."

"No, I want to hear you say it," she insisted.

"Okay. I had Coleridge do a little checking, 'cause I didn't buy that 'scared native girl' act, given how I've seen you handle yourself."

"Except when it came to flying."

"Yeah. Coleridge looked up some old *compadres* of ours who knew from the ground crew at your dad's private and very secure airfield that you saw him off, handing him a Father's Day gift with a nice bow on it."

Guzmán stared straight ahead.

"I know you killed your old man, Lina."

3:22pm
Sacramento

Dakin Saunders looked like a bigger prick in person than he did on his campaign posters. His face was stern, sallow, the gray eyes in the sunken brow glittering with a raptor's lust. His lips seemed always pinched together, as if a sour taste were permanently seared on his tongue. He was dressed in a gray Brooks Brothers suit and white shirt. The man's red-and-blue striped tie flapped as he walked rapidly along the hallway from his office in the State Capitol.

Flanked by his two special aides, he quickly strode away to avoid questions from several members of the Capitol press corp who had just come to see him.

"Attorney General Saunders," an eager young woman from the *Sacramento Bee* drilled him, "will you now verify or deny the rumor picked up by AP in the last hour that you offered a deal to known drug queen Lina Guzmán?"

One of the aides, a strawberry blonde cabana boy with narrow hips and wide shoulders, deflected that question. "The Attorney General has an important fund raiser he has to get to in Montecito."

3:23pm

Another reporter from a local TV station shouted as the three continued to walk away. "What about it, Mr. Saunders? Does this have anything to do with what are reputed attempts by you to shore up support within your own party? That, in fact, some party bigwigs are balking at your gubernatorial run?"

Saunders stopped and held up his hand as the second aide began to respond. "The real question, young man, is what are the members of my party afraid of, that they have trepidations in endorsing my candidacy? A candidacy that stands firm and forthright for keeping the family together, for the honor of our institutions, and for the duty to maintain our ways of life. Though we are engaged in a new kind of war in the Middle East, we are also more than three decades into another war you would do well to remember, a war that we cannot, indeed, must not lose either ... the War on Drugs.

"This most perfidious of scourges, this pharmaceutical terrorism that has claimed more American lives than terrorists ever have, will be routed. Its elimination is the cornerstone of my campaign." He paused, filled with his own sanctimony. "Not only did I not inhale, I never fired up.

"To the matter of drug sellers, slangers, or whatever your PC term is for them, I don't intend to give any one of them a free ride. Now, if one wants to voluntarily come forward and can provide credible, useful informa-tion leading to arrests and convictions, then there may be some room to negotiate their sentence. This is no different than what any prosecutor does on any given day. Thank you."

With that he turned and left the reporters. Saunders and his factotums walked down another hallway toward the security elevators leading to the underground parking structure for state officials. The dark-haired aide used his keys to unlock the secured elevator. The car came, and they entered.

"How the hell did this leak out?" He snarled at the strawberry blonde as the elevator descended.

The blonde animated his hands. "There've been explosions up and down the state, property and lives lost, sightings of Guzmán. There was bound to be talk."

The elevator came to a stop. "This isn't our floor," the brunette announced. He reached into his inner jacket as the door opened.

Before the trio stood a tall man, a portion of his face hidden by a blood-soaked wrapping. This man listed slightly.

"Who the ... Samson?" Saunders said. "How'd you get in here? Did anybody see you?"

Strawberry blonde grabbed Twelvetrees and pulled him into the elevator. "You were told to keep your distance."

"And I was told this would be a win-win situation, as you *yanquis* like to say." Twelvetrees braced his body in a corner of the elevator like a boxer on his last legs. The elevator ride resumed.

The car jerked to another stop, and the doors opened. The dark-haired aide positioned his body to watch for any intruders and to prevent the automatic doors from closing. Strawberry Blonde stood behind Saunders. And the Attorney General of California, the highest law officer in the state, was all up in Samson Twelvetrees's face, one of the biggest gangsters in the world.

3:31pm

"You're the leak, aren't you?" Saunders could barely keep his cool.

Twelvetrees wasn't about to do the backdown. He pressed his fingertips into Saunders's chest. Blondie flinched, but Saunders shook his head for him to be cool.

"Marley set me up. The cops in L.A. had me, you understand, Saunders. That roughneck blew us up, killed or wounded my men. I had to give the cops something—I am a wanted man after all." He shoved past Saunders and his men and walked into the parking structure.

"So like a weak sister you blabbed how you've been supplying information to my office for years on your fellow drug lords." Saunders walked alongside

Twelvetrees, his two aides in step behind them. Their footfalls sounded hollow on the concrete.

"All to build you up from crummy city attorney in Bell Gardens to county D.A., state attorney general, next governor, then what, the White House?" He laughed loudly, then started coughing. "You're going to get me immunity, Saunders. I'm an asset. Isn't that the word you types use?"

"Get real, Twelvetrees." Saunders made a sign to his blonde staffer. They'd been walking toward Saunders's Crown Victoria. "Don't worry, I didn't say anything about how I've also been secretly funneling money to your campaign war chest." Twelvetrees leaned against the fender of the car, folding his arms. He managed a tight smile. "And certainly nothing about our other financial arrangements."

"That's good, Samson, very good." Saunders pressed close to the man, his hand extended. "We'll work this out yet." Twelvetrees also held out his hand, and Strawberry Blonde inserted a heater in the usurper's gut. Dark Hair hung back a few paces, guarding the proceedings.

Marley, dap in a gray Prada sharkskin suit, suddenly leaped from around a pillar. His heel caught Strawberry Blonde flush on the chin, and the aide pole-axed to the concrete floor. Dark Hair shifted his Sig Sauer P245 from Twelvetrees and pumped two at the expediter. But Marley had anticipated such a move and went into a dive and roll that brought him beside a late model Navajo SUV. Kevlar or not, his head was vulnerable.

From this vantage point, he could see Lina Guzmán sneaking up too. They'd gotten to Sacramento on time, and, even with beefed-up security, it wasn't too hard for him to get inside this parking structure, given his collection of very good fake IDs. Some research had uncovered the plate number on Saunders's car, and it checked out. He spotted a pen on the dash from Le Colonial, the same kind he'd taken off the knife man in TJ. Not wanting any more surprises, Marley and Lina had hidden to see what was what.

Strawberry Blonde was stirring, and Dark Hair was crouched, momentarily concentrating on getting a shot off at Marley's legs.

"Hey *conyo*," Twelvetrees grinned wickedly as Dark Hair turned. "Don't ever turn your back on a wounded wolf, boy." He buried a blade in the side of Dark Hair's neck. Blood sprayed and splattered Twelvetrees's singed suede jacket, and the man was dead by the time he fell on his side.

3:39pm

Twelvetrees grabbed the dead aide's gun, then taunted Saunders. "Think I'd come here unarmed, motherfuckah?" He moved in on the crooked politician.

Strawberry Blonde was active and crabbed forward. He got his arms around Twelvetrees, upsetting the man's balance.

Saunders was about to bounce, but Guzmán wasn't having it.

"You crazy bitch, get the fuck out of my way!" he screamed. The Attorney General swung, his blow connecting with her jaw. Guzmán took the punch and countered with a hook to his jaw. That brought him up short, and she bopped him with a swift right. Saunders flopped on his ass, and, before he could cry "mama," she'd kicked him square in the head. The chump wilted.

Twelvetrees was pistol whipping Strawberry Blonde like he stole something from the drug lord's grandmother. He was having too much fun as he bent over his fragged opponent, the other man grasping Twelvetrees's pants legs.

"Please," he pleaded.

"That's right, beg. Bitch." Methodically, he brought the butt of the gun down again to sate his bloodlust.

"That's enough," Marley said. He grabbed the drug lord and pulled him off his practice dummy.

"Don't worry, I've got plenty left for you, homeboy." With part of his face covered in stained gauze, and his eyeballs doing the wild thing, Twelvetrees was like some escapee from Batman's rogue gallery. The Sig clicked, and Marley tucked his head behind his forearms as he threw them up. The bullets ripped into his upper arms and he spun away, partly from impact and partly by design.

"What the fuck?" Twelvetrees said, noting that Marley wasn't bleeding. "Must be some kind of chain mail woven into your suit."

"Good guess." Lina Guzmán had retrieved the gun from Strawberry Blonde and smoked off two rounds at

Twelvetrees. But a news van had just careened into the parking structure, and the hot ones blazed into it. The pretty boy newsman inside the vehicle—an aging surfer-type named Kelly Drier—screamed like a little girl. The driver, shook up like he was trapped in an episode of *Buffy*, plowed the ride into a new Lexus. The luxury car's alarms wailed as Twelvetrees scuttled into the regular passenger elevator and the doors closed.

"I ain't come this far to get punked." Marley took off.

"Be careful, baby." Guzmán called out to him as cops and civilians seeped into the parking structure.

Marley took the stairwell, hopping two at a time. He sprinted into the grand foyer, the fire door banging open. The digital readout over the elevator bay told him it was still heading up. He took the wide expanse of carpeted stairs inside the Capitol and followed the elevator to the third story where it could rise no higher.

Twelvetrees was three steps ahead of him when Marley cleared the stairwell. Without looking around, Twelvetrees fired blindly over his shoulder. People yelled and ducked, and the gang chieftain made it to another doorway. Marley had studied a layout of the Capitol on his Palm m515 as they drove to the location earlier. Those stairs

were for service personnel and led to the inner upper tier
of the dome itself. A man in overalls sped from that
direction.

3:48pm

He didn't break stride as he gobbled up the distance to
the door and went in and up. Marley slowed as he got

higher, the curvature of the fluted dome beginning
to loom over him like a concrete sky. He could hear
Twelvetrees's feet echoing on metal near him. Sheets of
plywood and sheetrock leaned against the wall next to
some tools, a sure sign of ongoing remodeling. He went
on and came across an access ladder leading to
a slot that opened onto the sloping roof. The desperate
gangster was on the ladder. He spotted Marley and took
a shot that puffed out plaster dust as the round buried
itself at Marley's foot. Twelvetrees went out onto the
roof.

Marley hung back. He took off his jacket and held it
over his head while he used his other hand to climb the
ladder. Several shots rained down on him. Twelvetrees
leaned into the opening, shooting. One of them went
past the partial protection and singed a path across his
leg. His side was bleeding too, but so what?

He reached up and got hold of Twelvetrees's ankle,
yanking hard.

This action tripped the gangster up, and he had to
windmill his arms to keep from toppling off the roof.
Marley scrambled onto the roof, the wind kicking up
from the east.

Overhead, a police helicopter swooped into place. A voice echoed over the chopper's loudspeaker. "You two come down now, that's an order."

Down below, a crowd including several news outlets had gathered. A recovered Kelly Drier, face ashen but blonde

locks in place, was at the front, jabbering away on his mike as his camerawoman aimed her minicam.

"While you fed information to Saunders, he protected you." Marley steadied himself on the dome.

"Oh well, Marley." The hammer of his gun dropped on an empty chamber. He tossed the gun away and clambered upward toward the peak using his hands and feet. The sectioned pole that held the American and Californian flags aloft was in pieces on the dome. Evidently repair work was being done on the shaft. Twelvetrees grabbed the end with the spear-like tip.

He slipped but still pointed the dangerous end at Marley.

"Come on, you cunning bastard, come on and take it."

He made a thrust, but Marley went flat and slithered out of the way. Twelvetrees's momentum carried him dangerously close to the edge.

"You ain't so bad now, are you?" Twelvetrees giggled— pain and the impending certainty of the gas chamber making him nut up.

"You're played, Twelvetrees." Marley was up, crimping his toes through his shoes to afford him a better grip. It didn't hurt that he had all his shoes fitted with non-skid soles.

"Whatever." Twelvetrees swung heavy like Barry Bonds and caught Marley off guard. The tip of the flag zipped past him, catching the side of his face. Marley reeled, his back arching away from his waist, and he could feel gravity start to pull him off the damned roof. He put his left

3:57pm

foot behind him, skidding toward the edge once more.

"This is the end of your bitch ass, Marley." Twelvetrees plunged the staff at his gut, but the player was still in the game.

Marley latched onto the pole, using Twelvetrees's grip and weight on the other end as ballast.

"Let go."

Marley gave him a skull's grin. Hand-over-hand, he began to inch his way along the pole. One of the cops in the 'copter had a high-powered rifle trained on them, but he had doubts. He wasn't sure which one to shoot. Marley had used an FBI ID to gain entrance to the parking structure. It corresponded to a real file buried in the Bureau's personnel computer. So as they sought to verify his bona fides, that bought him time.

And he was glad it wasn't an LAPD SWAT team— they'd light 'em both up and say sorry later.

Twelvetrees was shaking. "You *pinche bendejo*, Marley. You fucked everything up." He was sliding forward some as Marley kept coming, slow but steady.

"Just doing my job, chump."

"Fuck it then." Twelvetrees let go of the staff and stumbled toward the other man. Marley got him in a bear hug as Twelvetrees beat at him, screaming and crying. Using

Twelvetrees like a sawhorse in gymnastics, he vaulted past the man while pushing him away, toward the rim of the dome.

"Oh no," Twelvetrees said, grabbing at Marley's sleeve. "I'm not dying today."

Marley landed, but Samson Twelvetrees had a hand on his arm. He pulled.

"Scared, motherfuckah?"

"One of us should be." Marley did a roundhouse kick that connected alongside Twelvetrees's temple. He blinked rapidly and got all disoriented as his grip loosened.

"That all you got, punk?" The bandages had come undone and were skewed over his eyes. He had to reach up to clear his vision.

Marley was right up on him.

"Boo."

One punch, and Samson Twelvetrees, the baddest mutha with the coldest hook-up of dope in the western hemisphere, did an involuntary back somersault off the Capitol dome.

"Marleyyyy . . ." he wailed before he collided with the sidewalk. All the video cameras recorded his descent. Later, Fox would air a special about the Saunders-Twelvetrees conspiracy. A beautiful piano number was added to the slo-mo clip of Twelvetrees falling from the building.

Marley had slipped into the slot in the dome as cops came rushing up from below. He went behind some of the boards on the landing. In less than two minutes the police, bristling with nines, had thrown back the building materials, only to expose an air shaft minus its metal screen.

4:00pm

＊　＊　＊

A special commission appointed by the governor found that Saunders busted drug operations that Twelvetrees ratted out to make his reputation. And Twelvetrees got large and strong in the shadow of the lion, Lina Guzmán's father. In a safe in an off-site office that Saunders maintained, all sorts of incriminating evidence, including copiously ledgered accounting books, were found. In the mix were DEA surveillance photos of Lina Guzmán kissing her *papá* while she handed him a gift.

At a swank hotel in Newport Beach, Marley and Guzmán met over dinner. She too had gotten away amid the chaos in the garage as the press descended on a dazed Saunders.

Marley tasted his wine, but the fine vintage was bitter in his mouth.

"He made you the offer after Twelvetrees started actin' ill to make sure you didn't tell anybody what you knew. This far into the governor's race, he had to make sure nothing of his connection to Twelvetrees got tipped. Once you went for the supposed deal, those two were gonna make sure you got chilled. Everybody knew Twelvetrees had ordered the hit. Afterward, Saunders would arrange some kind of accident to silence him. He'd be set."

Guzmán caressed his hand. "Let's go up to the room I've gotten for us here. I want to massage you in the Jacuzzi."

He looked at her evenly. "I'd like nothing better, Lina. But you iced your own father."

"I told you, he was a devil."

"That could be. But the fact remains you got phat off of what you did."

"I'm going legit, you know that."

"Yeah, yeah," he nodded. "I know what I hear, Lina. And I hear you're buying into high tech firms and so forth, but that isn't different than what the old school, the mob, has been doing for years."

"You can share it all with me, Marley."

He stroked her cheek. "I'm tempted."

His hand remained on her face, their eyes absorbing each other. Then he got up and walked out. She lowered her head as he went.

By the time the press was through with him, Saunders was toast. He was facing hard time by a pitiless jury and a no-nonsense judge, the same judge Saunders had aggressively pushed for his appointment by the governor less than two years before. But Saunders wasn't down with a 6-by-8 existence. He tried to sneak away to London and wound up in a shootout with some security personnel. He finally made the big time; video shots of his corpse were played on all the news shows. Rumor was that Gene Hackman would get the role of Saunders in the movie.

An anonymous donor sent a donation to rebuild the ruined rec center in South Park.

And Marley got paid in full. The expediter received a cash delivery covering his expenses and his balance. He spent a few days in Reno, drinking single malt, gambling badly, and trying to forget.

Acknowledgements

The history of this novel is somewhat torturous and involved. It began as a project for another outfit that is now defunct. While spinning the yarn of Marley, Lina, et al. for this entity, it became clear that I had a different idea what this story was about, and how it should be told, than the editor-publisher of this house had. And so *The Perpetrators* was kicked to the curb after several go-rounds with this company. But thanks to the gents of UglyTown, and their patience and advice to see me through a cohesive rewrite, the results are in your hands. For good or bad, this is the story and the style I wanted to tell it in.